MY BEST FRIEND'S SECRET

CRYSTAL LACY

My Best Friend's Secret

Edit & proofing by DJ Jamison

Cover by Crystal Lacy

DEAR READER:

This story contains scenes with exhibitionism, voyeurism, and multiple partners. If any of this is not to your tastes, please try some of my other books instead. Thank you!

PROLOGUE - RAYSEN

Thanksgiving

THE SIGHT OF YUKI MIURA, face lightly stubbled and wearing the old Atlas of Law Student Brain T-shirt I got him for Christmas our first year in the apartment together, makes my heart contract with happiness. It also makes me squint at him in surprise.

"What're you doing here?"

Yuki laughs and pushes past me, his hand warm against my arm as he moves me out of the doorway to let himself in. "Coming to help wrestle the turkey into the pan, of course," he announces loudly.

Squeals of delight erupt around the room as all three of my sisters—traitors, the lot of them—rush to hug Yuki and tell him how much they've missed him since the last family dinner he attended. Now that he's a law associate, Yuki's time is at a premium, and he can't always make it to the monthly family dinners at my parents' place.

He wasn't supposed to make it tonight for Thanksgiving, either. Maybe he still isn't.

Thankfully, before I need to ask, my mom enters the living room and, after enveloping Yuki in a hug of her own, asks, "What are you doing here?"

Yuki casts an amused glance my way. "I'm beginning to think I'm not welcome. That's the second time I've been asked that."

Mama frowns. "You know we always want you, and Raymond will be glad to not have to help me lift the turkey out of the brine." We all know my dad has a thing against touching raw meat of any kind, and always grumbles after having to handle the turkey on Thanksgiving. Since I don't like it either, we all very gratefully pawned the task off on Yuki from his very first Thanksgiving spent with us and never looked back.

"But seriously," I say, trying not to think too much about how many Thanksgivings Yuki's spent with us, and how many more I *want* him to spend with us, as part of the family. As part of *me*. "I thought you were hanging with Gray today. I told Mama as much." I try to keep my voice as level as can be, so it's not completely obviously just how much I dislike the idea of Yuki spending Thanksgiving with his boyfriend. We're best friends. I should be *glad* Yuki is getting close enough to his boyfriend to want to spend holidays together like any normal lovers would.

Instead, the thought of losing Thanksgiving together makes something go dry and twisted in my stomach. So much so that I've had to hide my unhappiness all day behind a veneer of cheerfulness that I'm not sure has fooled anyone.

"We got into it last night." Yuki shrugs. "He asked for some space, so I figured I might as well come over here and help out. Besides, I couldn't pass up Mama's pumpkin crunch."

We wander into the kitchen together, and Yuki opens the fridge to grab the container the turkey has been brined in, lifting it with a grunt to set on the kitchen counter. As he casts a glance around the kitchen in search of the roasting pan, I turn the oven on to preheat. We've done this enough times before that it feels like breathing.

"So," I say slowly, unable to keep my mouth shut. I shouldn't be prying into Yuki's relationships, but I find myself doing it anyway. "What did you guys fight about?"

Yuki shrugs, pulling on kitchen gloves as I grab the bottom of the container to hold it in place. The turkey fits super snug inside, and we discovered pretty quickly that if someone *doesn't* hold the container while you're trying to extract it, disaster can happen. No one wants to spend Thanksgiving scrubbing the floors of raw turkey juices.

"He asked me to move in with him."

I feel a pang in my chest at the words. "Oh," is all I manage to say.

"And I told him I'd think about it."

"Oh," I repeat. I always knew this moment would come eventually. It's not like it's even *normal* for two guys in their mid-twenties to still be living together. After we finished school and both got jobs, it was only a matter of time before one of us moved out.

Yuki grunts as he lifts the turkey and deposits it cleanly onto the roasting pan. I snag a few paper towels and dab at the raw bird to get rid of some of the brine, before remembering we were supposed to put it into the sink to rinse off first.

So much for having done this enough times it feels like breathing. Guess we're both a little distracted. And really, I've kind of got the breath knocked out of me by Yuki's announcement. *Breathing*—or at least breathing normally—has suddenly become a problem.

"He didn't like that answer," Yuki continues. "Said he thought I'd be happy he asked, but I just looked like a deer in the headlights."

I manage a soft chuckle. "Did you?"

"How the hell was I supposed to know? It's not like I was looking in the mirror when he told me."

"Were you? Happy he asked?" *Do you want to move in with him?*

I hate how long Yuki doesn't answer my question. I hate it even more when he just sighs and goes to the sink to wash his hands, turning his back to me. "Let's not talk about this right now. I want to enjoy Thanksgiving, not dwell on Gray's weird tantrum."

Since I'm supposed to be his friend, *just* his friend who shouldn't care so deeply about whether he's going to move in with his boyfriend or not, I change the subject. Not because I'm as reluctant to hear Yuki's answer as he apparently is to give it. "Mama says she's not making pumpkin crunch this year."

An audible gasp escapes Yuki. "*What?*" he exclaims, spinning around to face me, his eyes wide with dismay. "Why not?"

"Well, it's your favorite, and she didn't think you were coming, so." I shrug, trying to keep a straight face as Yuki's mouth falls open. I can't ignore the tug of a smile trying to break free at the corners of my mouth, though, and he's too familiar with all my facial expressions to not catch it. His eyes narrow, and he steps closer to me, pointing an accusing finger at my chest.

"You're a dirty liar who lies, Raysen. Where is the pumpkin crunch? I didn't see it in the fridge."

I laugh. "In the crisper drawer. Mama didn't want it accidentally getting smooshed when we moved the turkey."

"That turkey. Always a menace."

"Amen." I grin when Yuki turns to the fridge and pulls open the door to check that the pumpkin crunch is, indeed, in the crisper drawer. God, he's adorable. Adorable and gorgeous and funny. Smart. Just. Perfect.

And someone else's. I wish I didn't have to keep reminding myself of the fact. What is *wrong* with me?

"Okay, before we continue with the epic food prep, we're going to make coffee," Yuki announces, reaching for the coffee pot where it sits on one of the high cupboards.

"Because heaven forbid that you not have at least four cups of coffee before noon on any given day," I say.

"Amen," he says as I hand him the coffee canister.

THE IMPENDING CHANGE to our roommates status causes a heavy weight in my stomach that persists for the next few hours as we all help my mom prepare for Thanksgiving dinner. Since it's going to be our family, my aunt and her family, including a gaggle of cousins and their kids, plus a few of my dad's old tennis buddies, we have a whole lot of food to prepare before the crowd arrives at six for Thanksgiving dinner. At least the peeling of potatoes and various other veggies and legumes distracts me from the conversation we didn't finish.

Of course, it doesn't take all day to prepare with all five of us kids helping. After washing up and filling Yuki up with even more coffee, we do what we usually do when we're back at my parents' place and find ourselves with an hour or two free. We walk out to the old tennis court by my elementary school to rally balls back and forth.

The walk takes under ten minutes, and in those minutes I think back to the first time we walked down to the court, on the Black Friday after our first Thanksgiving together. We spent the previous day and most of Friday morning holed up in my room and were basically ready to get out of the house. Yuki was pretty terrible at first, but it was nice to see him concentrating on hitting the soft balls I was aiming at him and forgetting all the crap that had just transpired with his family that week. As the years went on, it became our routine.

The tennis court, like our apartment, is *our* space. It makes me feel connected to Yuki when I stand on the cracked concrete and look at him over the sagging net lines.

"Ready to get your ass kicked?" Yuki calls out, his habitual grin lighting up his face.

"Sure, Miura. Sure." We both know I'm a better tennis player than Yuki, especially now that I've bulked up a little and am not the scrawny kid I was when we first started doing this. I've been playing longer, since my dad is really into it, and while Yuki's a lot better than when he first started, the gap between our experiences is just too high. Which is why we only rally casually instead of playing real games. It isn't actually *about* winning anything for either of us. It's just a way to get our blood pumping and our bodies moving, clear our minds of everything except the pop of the ball against the racket and the zoom of the next return as it sails over the net.

We play until we're both sweaty and exhausted, then sit on the rickety old court bench together, our thighs nearly touching. The smell of Yuki's sweat and mine mingling in the air, the warmth of his body so close like this, keeps me on the edge. If I focus on any of the details for too long, I'm sure I'll sprout a boner.

I'm distracted from my own unwanted arousal by Yuki's voice, so low it's almost inaudible. "I didn't really need to think about it."

"About what?" I ask, even though I pretty much *knew* the instant I made out his words. Of course I do. I haven't really stopped thinking about it all day.

"Moving in with Gray. I told him I'd think about it, but I already know I'm going to tell him no."

The overwhelming relief I feel is like a physical ache in my chest, and I have to fight to keep my expression outwardly impassive. I don't know if it actually works. "If you're not ready, you're not ready."

"He's going to be even more pissed. But yeah, I'm not ready for that with him yet. Plus I don't want to just up and leave you with half the rent to pay."

"I could probably find someone else," I say, because what *else* am I supposed to say? *Please don't leave me, I won't be able to find anyone that's you?* No. This has been a long time coming. Yuki and I decided long ago that our friendship was more important than any gratification we could find in each other's bodies, and I'm convinced I'm just not his type anyway. If it hasn't happened in our six years of friendship, it's never happening. Which is why I need to be strong about it. Rip it off like a Band-Aid and get over these *feelings* I have for my best friend.

Maybe I just need to schedule another session with Dominic and one of his friends. Hell, maybe *all* of them. It's been a few months since I've seen any of them, and it's not like the last time distracted me more than a few days from my feelings for Yuki. But it's still worth a try. Right now, I need the uncomplicated release that a night with Dominic provides.

"Maybe I *like* living with you," Yuki mutters, bringing me back to the present.

Any thoughts of seeing Dominic again sinks into the background. I can't deny the words are like catnip for my soul. "It's only because I start your coffee machine in the morning and don't complain about your horrible habit of leaving books all over the living room floor."

"Much. You don't complain *much*."

"I'm a saint."

"You kind of are." He tosses me a fond smile that makes something twist in my chest. The sun's setting, and the light hits his hair, picking up the highlights and making him glow. It takes all the self-control I have not to move forward and kiss him.

I glance away, shielding my eyes to look up into the sky. I can't make things awkward between us and ruin this. So we're not together. So I'll never get to kiss Yuki or hold him in my arms, or feel what it's like to have him inside me. At least we'll always have this. Friends don't break up. Friendship lasts forever. It's worth stifling the romantic feelings I have for Yuki if it means I get to have everything else.

I lean over to pick up my racket again. "Come on. Sun's setting. Let's go get some turkey."

We're nearly home when Yuki brushes his hair out of his eyes and asks, "You think Gray will cheer up if I bring him some pumpkin crunch tomorrow?"

My stomach sinks, although I don't know why. It's not like I'm rooting for Yuki and his boyfriend to break up. Of course not. I want Yuki to be happy, and I know it can't be with me. "I think it's definitely worth a try."

He smiles to himself, bumping shoulders with me as we rush through the front door. "Remind me to grab extra after dinner?"

I swallow. "Sure. I'll remind you."

I

YUKI

December 28th

The shower opens and lets out a cloud of steam, the scent of Raysen's citrusy shampoo filling the entire apartment in its wake. I glance up from my book just in time to catch a glimpse of him as he strolls into his room, clad only in a towel around his waist. Wet dark hair, water glistening on his tanned skin, toned back muscles flexing as he walks.

I turn my gaze resolutely back to the book. *Stop checking out your best friend!* I admonish myself. Clearly my breakup with Gray—and the resulting dry spell—has turned me into a horndog. It hasn't even been that long since we broke up, only three weeks, and I've already gone back to salivating after Raysen.

Maybe instead of catching up on the adventures of MurderBot tonight, I should hit a club. Find someone to scratch that itch. *Not* fantasize about my roommate's round, perfect ass and what it would look like sans towel. I had the chance to find out freshman year of college and I chose to stay friends, instead.

Best decision I could've made, considering we're still tight and still living together after six years. I'm not going to ruin the most important thing in my life just for some ass. Not even if it *is* Raysen's ass.

I'm pulling up my phone and debating whether I should redownload Grindr when Raysen comes back out, dressed in black jeans and a white T-shirt. Pretty standard outfit for him, except he's also wearing the expensive cologne I stupidly got him for his birthday this year which makes him smell like sex.

"You going out?" I ask, raising an eyebrow.

Raysen clears his throat and scratches at the side of his stubbled face. A *clear* tell he's stalling for time. "Uh, yeah. Sort of."

"Sort of?" I tease. "You've got a date or something?" You'd think Raysen would be playing the field more, with his good looks, but in the six years we've been friends, he's only brought a handful of guys home. Most weekends, he's here in the apartment, playing video games or working on his own game designs. So it's good that he's going out. It's about time he meets someone. What has it been—seven months since he's had a date?

Not that anyone's keeping count.

"Not really." There's that scratch again. "Just going to a house party. I'd invite you, but the guy's kind of weird about strangers."

"It's fine. I'm probably going to be heading out of here soon, too. I need to get laid yesterday."

"Right, getting laid. Sounds good." Something flickers in Raysen's eyes, but he glances away before I can pinpoint what it is. "I've just got to find where I stashed my keys and wallet," he mumbles.

"Oh, they're in the kitchen, by the mail. I saw them when I was grabbing a coffee."

"Oh, thanks." His amused voice drifts out from the kitchen. "How many coffees have you had already? Four?"

"Five."

"Caffeine junkie."

"Hey," I say, waggling my eyebrows when he emerges from the kitchen with his keys and wallet in one hand. "I'll be the one laughing when you're passed out at eleven p.m. and I'm still at the club scoring ass at two in the morning."

Raysen's eye-roll is expansive. "I'll be ready in the morning for your epic crash," he says, giving me a mock-salute before he heads for the door. When he leaves, I close my eyes and inhale deeply, taking in the scent of the sex cologne mixed in with the shampoo, both of which still lingers in the air.

I stand and walk toward the bathroom. No time like the present to get ready to head out myself. If Raysen's going to have fun tonight, shouldn't I have fun too?

I'm walking to my car when I spot Raysen leaning on the hood of his, typing on his phone. When he sees me, he mutters something under his breath and gives a nod in my direction.

"What's the matter?" I ask when I approach. "I thought you were headed somewhere."

"I was." Raysen makes a face. "Car's fucked. Couldn't get it to start."

I sigh. "That sucks." I refrain from telling Raysen he really should replace that piece-of-shit death trap with something that doesn't break down every other full moon. "Need a lift?"

Raysen glances at his phone again. In the dim lighting of the streetlamps, I think I see him flushing. "I'm waiting for an Uber. Says it's ten minutes away."

"How far?"

"Wahiawa," he mumbles.

"On an Uber? Isn't that expensive as fuck?"

He shrugs. "At this point, I figured it was better than being later than I already am."

"Just cancel it. I'll take you. Honestly, you could've called and asked."

"Didn't want to disturb your night when you're going on the prowl," Raysen says, following me to my car.

"Five coffees' worth of clubbing, remember? I can afford to start my night a little later."

"Oh, yeah. I remember."

Raysen navigates while I take us to the house in Wahiawa, which is in a neighborhood I don't *really* want to drop him off at, but what the hell. The house is nice enough, with white-washed walls that have seen some wear and well-tended plants out front.

"This the place?"

"Yeah, I think so." Then he actually flips down the visor in the passenger seat and checks his reflection in the mirror. There's tension in his shoulders, and he lets out a long exhale as he stares the mirror down.

"So this *isn't* a date."

To my surprise, he laughs. "Yeah, no. Definitely not a date. But thanks for worrying about my virtue."

"I wasn't." I doth protest too much.

"I know." He clears his throat, flashing me a grateful smile. "Thanks for the ride. You saved me thirty bucks."

"How're you getting home, though?"

"Uh. I'll catch a ride from someone. Or do the Uber."

"You can call me."

Raysen gives me a skeptical look. "What, and interrupt you with a hookup? No, thanks. I'll be fine." He says the last sentence like it should have a *Mom* attached to it, and I feel a spark of irritation.

The thing is, I'm sure he'll be fine, too. When we first met

Raysen hadn't yet hit his full growth spurt yet and was scrawny as fuck. Now, we go to the gym together more often than not, and he's slender but wiry with muscle. He's strong. With those kickboxing classes he goes to, I know he can take care of himself. No reason to be overprotective of him.

So I let him go, sending him off with a quick wave. I don't wait to see him getting into the house, because I know he'll probably think I'm babying him again if I do.

It's just difficult not to worry about Raysen. He's always been so... *fragile* is the only word I can think of, really. Shy and timid and too fucking sweet for his own good.

I sigh, thunking the back of my head against the seat when I'm at the next stop light. I *really* need to get laid so I can start remembering that I shouldn't think of my best friend as anything other than a friend. None of this *too fucking sweet* crap.

A mute beep catches my attention, and I scan the car for it. My eyes land on the shiny screen of Raysen's phone, with a random social media news update flicking over the top of the screen. I sigh, shaking my head and chuckling. Of course he'd forget his phone on the one night he'll probably need it to call for an Uber home. Well, at least I'm only a few minutes away.

I make a U-turn as soon as I'm able and head back toward the house, parking on the side of the road and walking to the front door. At least, I *think* it's the right house. I ring the doorbell, and then, when no one comes to answer after a minute, ring it again.

"Coming," a muffled male voice comes from the other side. A minute later, a tall man opens the door. He's got dark brown hair and sparkling blue eyes a shade darker than Raysen's baby blues. The guy gives me a once-over, and then he licks his lips, smiling. "Well, hello."

"Uh," I say, taken aback by the lustful gleam I see in his

gaze. "I'm here for Raysen. His—" I'm about to say his phone's right in my pocket, when the guy steps closer and claps a hand on my shoulder, drawing me past the threshold and into the house. It happens so quickly that I don't have a chance to react before the door closes behind me.

"I'm Dominic," the man says, those blue eyes still openly assessing me. "So, you're a friend of Ray-Boy, huh?"

Ray-Boy? I think. I consider being offended on Raysen's behalf for such a lame nickname, but then the guy steps back and strips off his T-shirt. My mouth goes dry, because he's *ripped*, and something about the way he's looking at me right now, like he's weighing me up, is sexy as fuck. No wonder Raysen was so stoked about this party. So, yeah, all I manage to croak out is a raspy, "Yup."

He steps close. The movement brings to my attention his legs, which then brings to my attention his jeans and the huge bulge that's now visible at the crotch since he doesn't have his T-shirt hiding anything. I feel my dick perking up in interest at the sight.

Dominic just gives me a knowing look and grins, baring straight white teeth. "You want a drink, or are you ready to go in back?" he asks, pointing to a kitchen peeking out from the other side of the house, then nodding in the direction of a darkened hallway.

"The back?" I'm assuming that's where Raysen is. Except, who the fuck knows? This guy is half-naked and hard, and he's offering to take me places. Is it wrong of me to seriously consider going wherever that is? Because it really *has* been too long since the last time my cock has seen any action other than my hand sliding over it, and I really, really need to stop checking Raysen out.

Dominic leads me down a hallway, past several closed bedroom doors. Some of them have lights shining from underneath the doors, and some of them are pitch dark, but with voices sounding on the other side.

"I usually don't let strange guys in, but since you've got good references—" at this he actually glances back and tosses a wink at me— "... I'm gonna let it slide." The way he says the word *slide* is almost pornographic. Maybe it's just my imagination?

As soon as we step into the last bedroom and I see three other guys standing around, their jeans pushed down past their asses, their hands busily stroking their hard cocks, I'*m fairly certain* it's not my imagination.

"What the fuck?" I mutter, mouth going dry and my cock plumping up even further when I spot what's on the opposite wall. "Is that ... ?"

"Your dirtiest fantasy come true?" comes a quiet murmur close to my ear from beside me. Shit, even Dominic's voice is sexy, all smooth, silky baritone. "Yes."

Well, no, I think to myself. I've never actually fantasized about this *exact* thing, and it's probably not the *dirtiest* I can come up with, but goddamn, it's close. There's a cardboard wall where the door to what is probably the bathroom should be, attached to the door frame with layers upon layers of duct tape. There's also a hole, positioned approximately at crotch level, carved into the cardboard, with duct tape to smooth out the edges. Above the hole are the words *Insert Cock Here* written in permanent marker, with arrows pointing down.

Just as my brain catches up to what's really happening in this room, the tall black dude with shiny bars pierced through his nipples flashes the entire room a grin and pumps his cock once, then walks toward the glory hole, aiming his cock toward the opening.

"Is there a... Is someone on the other side?" I whisper to Dominic. I realize Dominic's got his arm draped around my shoulders, like he's scared I might bolt if he's not holding onto me. I feel the arm stiffen for a split-second, then soft laughter against my ear.

"Shit," he mutters ruefully. "I think you're lost, bro. You want to get out of here?"

I arch an eyebrow at him, but my attention is still on the guy with his dick in the hole, who's drawing his hips back, revealing the shiny, spit-slick base of his cock. "Holy fuck," I croak. "Someone's on the other side."

Dominic's eyes give this weird flutter, and then he squeezes my shoulder with his hand almost bracingly and walks me closer to the cardboard wall. "Yeah," he says. "It's our very own DIY glory-hole. Normally it's made of plywood board, but someone borrowed our usual board at the last party and hasn't given it back yet, so." He nods down at the cardboard construction. "This'll do."

Tall Dude groans and thrusts his hips, driving his cock deeper into the hole. "Fuck, yes, it'll do," he mutters. He braces his hands on either side of the door frame for leverage and pumps his hips into the waiting mouth on the other side. A wet, choking sound follows a particularly deep thrust, and that has my cock rock hard in my pants. The other guys, their cocks already bare, seem to be in similar states.

I glance curiously down at Dominic, and *yeah*, it's a pleased crowd all around right now. He catches me looking and shoots me a grin, leaning in close enough to whisper.

"Good show, huh? You want to give yourself some love, feel free to whip it out. I promise no one will mind."

My throat goes dry at the thought of undoing my jeans and taking out my cock, right here, in front of four literal strangers. I don't even know the other guys' names. It should freak me out, but it only arouses me.

When I unzip and release my cock, Dominic lets out a crow of appreciation.

"I love an uncut cock," he growls into my ear, making me shiver. "Bet he does, too."

He. The man behind the cardboard barrier. The one who's now making wet, dirty noises with his mouth as he swallows down that thick cock. *God, that's hot.*

I stroke myself, my eyes glued to the shiny length of Tall Dude's cock as it pistons in and out of the hole. I imagine the guy on the other side, on his knees, mouth open wide, lips shiny with saliva and precum as he gags on that monster cock.

It doesn't take long for him to finish off the Tall Dude, who cries out and tips his head back, jerking his hips so hard the duct tape on the doorframe squeaks and the cardboard nearly disengages from it. "Fuck yeah, take it," he mutters, moaning as he pulls his cock free, a bead of cum still welling up from the tip.

"Shit," Dominic sighs, moving from his position beside me to grab a roll of duct tape from a side table. "Matt, come hold it for me while I retape?"

They layer on the tape quickly and efficiently, taking care to test the cardboard barrier with their hands before stepping back.

"I think you've earned the honors," Dominic tells the guy named Matt, grinning at him, and Matt takes position in front of the glory hole, inserting his cock with a low grunt. I watch, mesmerized, as he thrusts in hard and deep right away, listening to the guy on the other side choke again.

Meanwhile, the first guy has slumped onto the bed, his chest heaving as he recovers from what looked like an epic orgasm.

"You going to stick around for the finale, Mitch?" Dominic asks him.

At Dominic's question, Mitch's eyes fly open, and he makes a small *pfft* noise. "Hell, yeah. Just need some recovery time. Gimme half an hour. *Shit,* his mouth was so fucking hot. It's like he was made to suck dick."

The comment makes heat flood my body as I think about

how the guy on the other side of the barrier can probably hear him saying that. I wonder how it makes him feel, knowing his skills are so appreciated. Knowing this guy thinks he's made for cock-sucking.

We continue to watch, sans Mitch, as Matt has his turn. The muscles of his ass bunch and flex as he thrusts enough to rattle the cardboard. I wish I could see the other side of it, see the hot mouth swallowing him down, taking all of these cocks without a word of complaint. In fact, the guy seems to enjoy the throat-fucking he's getting from Matt, because I can hear him moaning in the back of his throat. It's so hot. I don't know how I'm going to last until—

Until what? Until it's my turn? Am I seriously considering letting a stranger suck me off?

Okay, yes. I seriously am. How can anyone resist, who's seen these guys' faces as they're being serviced?

"Here it comes," Matt warns, after what seems like an *hour* of face-fucking but is probably more like fifteen minutes. He makes a few quick, erratic thrusts into the hole, and then he withdraws, still pumping his leaking cock.

"Next. Lito?" Dominic says, and the last guy, a shorter Filipino dude with a disproportionately long cock, eases his way in. He's gentler than either of the other two, crooning soft, slightly accented words to the guy on the other side, telling him what a good boy he is and how he's going to make him feel so good later.

"Later?" I whisper to Dominic, since he's clearly the one in charge of the show.

"Maybe," he answers, in the same volume. "We had some plans to let our lovely tribute out and give him a good pounding, but..." He shrugs. "I don't know if it's in the cards now." He gives me an assessing look. "Are you going to stick around and take your turn?"

"I don't know." I *want* to, but I don't want to make the other guy uncomfortable, either. It seems like all of these guys know each other pretty well, and here I am, a complete stranger. "Would it bother him since I'm a complete stranger?"

Dominic laughs softly, eyes widening inexplicably for a second. He shakes his head, his gaze flicking to Lito as the other man groans loudly and slumps against the doorframe. "Hell, no. It won't bother him. Why do you think that glory hole is there? He gets off on the fantasy of us all being strangers."

I guess that makes sense. Otherwise, why go through the trouble of setting up something like that, with duct tape and cardboard, of all things? I clear my throat. "Cool. That sounds good."

Dominic laughs and whips his cock out. It's thick and veiny, and long but not *too* long. He gives it a few lazy strokes, and then approaches the vacated glory hole, tapping his fingers playfully against the cardboard before trailing them down and sticking two into the hole. "This mouth ready for my cock?" he asks, clearly not expecting an answer, because his fingers are pumping in and out, and all anyone can hear are the soft, wet sounds of sucking and licking as the guy on the other side devours his fingers.

I bite back a moan of my own when he finally pulls his fingers free and replaces them with his cock. Compared to the other three guys, Dominic's relatively still, barely moving his body at all. He just leans against the cardboard barrier, one arm propped almost carelessly against the frame, his cock shoved to the hilt into the hole. He doesn't dirty talk, only hums in approval when something especially good happens, and *presses* himself more firmly against the barrier. It should be boring to watch, but somehow it's more arresting than all the others.

Matt, who seemed to have wandered out of the room, comes back in carrying a six-pack of cream soda, one of which he offers to me. "Best to stay hydrated," he says, flashing me a friendly grin. I wave off the soda, partially because I'm not sure I *need* to stay hydrated. Not sure I'm engaging in whatever this is.

An orgy. An orgy *is what this is, Miura. For fuck's sake.*

Of course, everyone else has a soda. Even Dominic, who finishes with a low groan and tucks himself back into his pants, then immediately reaches for a bottle. After a quick sip, he crouches down and speaks directly into the hole, in a low, hushed tone so I can't make out what he's saying. He *does* glance quickly at me before whispering something else to the guy on the other side. And then he stands again and faces me.

"It's up to you if you want to stay," he tells me. "Whatever you decide, it was hot having you here, watching." Grinning, he inclines his head toward the glory hole. "For all of us."

Murmurs of agreement echo around the room, and I'm suddenly deeply aware of my cock still hanging out of my boxers, hard enough to pound nails. Blood racing in my veins, I step forward, gripping myself in one hand as I brace against the doorframe with the other.

First time for everything, right?

I *was* going to check out a club or two and find a hookup to scratch my itch. This is kind of the same thing. Except infinitely kinkier. Hotter, too.

I don't know if it's because I'm new, and the other guys are just curious, or maybe it's because they've all come already, but the four of them crowd around me, looking on as I feed my cock into the hole.

Nothing happens for a moment, just cool air on my sensitive skin. Then his warm breath is on me, followed by the hot tip of his tongue at the base of my cock, running up the underside. He licks me all over, like he's memorizing the taste and feel of me. It feels good, and I let him tease me for a while before I give an impatient jerk of my hips.

Hands curl firmly around the base of my cock, and finally, his mouth closes over the head, tongue slipping under the foreskin to get at the skin underneath before flattening out so he can take me in. And *fuck*, does that feel good. It's been too long, and his mouth is so good—hot suction milking my cock as he bobs an inch and then pulls back before advancing again. My cock takes small dips into his mouth, then surfaces, then goes for a deep dive. The erratic tempo makes me nearly dizzy with pleasure. Makes it impossible for me to predict what sensations I'll feel next.

This close, I can hear wet *slap-slap*-ing sounds coming from the other side of the barrier, a steady thump following that same rhythm beating against the cardboard. I realize it's him touching himself, hand working his own cock as he blows me.

"Yeah. Jack yourself. Get yourself off while you suck it." *Shit, did I just say that out loud?*

Apparently so. The mouth on my cock pauses. A low moan vibrates around me. His hand falls away, and he moans again before sinking his mouth all the way down to the base, swallowing my cock whole. The slapping sound gets more intense and then stops abruptly. I can feel the sharp hisses of breath he's taking, his throat convulsing around me.

Holy shit. He's coming. This guy is blowing me and spraying cum all over the other side of this cardboard. With me in his mouth. With my taste on his tongue. The thought pushes me over the edge. I grip the doorframe tight as I orgasm, my cum shooting straight down his throat. He chokes on it, and I feel guilty for a split second until he swallows and moans again, pulling back to lick and suck at my softening cock, lavishing attention onto it.

I don't want it to end, even when I start to get oversensitive. I do pull back, though, because now that I'm not in the moment anymore, it occurs to me that I gripped the doorframe so tight, I tore off some of the duct tape, and the cardboard is attached to the door on just one side. It's liable to collapse at any moment.

Dominic rushes to the rescue, bracing the cardboard up with one arm. He's completely naked. I glance back and see all the other guys have gotten rid of the rest of their clothes as well. In my concentration, I didn't notice them moving away from me and taking up space on the bed. Matt and Mitch are sitting at the foot of the bed, necking, their bare cocks rubbing. Lito is splayed sideways on the other end, touching himself idly.

"You need more duct tape?" Matt calls, when he realizes what Dominic is doing.

Dominic seems to consider for a moment, then shakes his head. "I think it's time for the curtains-down portion of the evening, but let's check with our star performer and see, shall we?"

He pries half of the cardboard off the side of the door and laughs. "What a lovely mess you made." So I was right. He *did* come sucking my cock. I step back to give them some privacy as Dominic speaks to the guy on the other side in a low, hushed voice. I don't hear any replies back, but Dominic nods and turns to the rest of us.

"He's down for everything we discussed, but he wants a blindfold. Can you find me something from the nightstand, Lito?"

Lito opens a drawer on the nightstand and rummages inside. "Silk scarf or rope?"

"Scarf. It's hell to wash rope."

Lito pulls out a long black scarf and tosses it in our direction. I step forward to catch it, and hand it to Dominic, who flashes me a grateful smile.

"Come hold this for me?" he asks. "And don't peek yet, okay?" He pulls the rest of the tape off on one side of the door and steps inside, presumably to help 'our star performer' put the blindfold on. I keep the cardboard barrier propped up, feeling a little foolish. What am I still doing here? Am I really going to stay here and watch while everyone fucks this blindfolded guy?

Yes. Yes, you are.

This is hands-down the craziest thing I've ever done, but since I'm already doing it, might as well go all the way.

"Okay, he's ready," Dominic announces, popping his head back out. His eyes land on me, and there's a considering look in them that makes me unaccountably nervous. "Are *you* ready?" His eyes drift to each of the other guys, and I know he's asking all of us, not just me, but it certainly *feels* like he's talking to just me.

When he meets my gaze, I give a short nod. I palm my cock, which is already showing signs of life again. Mixed in with the nerves is a curious excitement to see what the guy who's made me come so hard looks like.

Dominic begins ripping the rest of the duct tape off. The cardboard barrier comes down, and I catch sight of the cum stains dotting the other side, just like I imagined. Then I glance up, my gaze landing on the man kneeling on the floor, naked and blindfolded. My breath catches in my throat, and I nearly stumble as shock propels me backward.

Oh, my God. This isn't really happening. It can't be happening.

"I've got to get out of here," I blurt.

I'm already trying to block this out of my mind, to go back to *before* tonight, when I hadn't had my cock deep in my best friend's mouth, pumping my cum down his throat. Because the naked guy who's been servicing all of us tonight? He's Raysen. My roommate. The guy I've shared my life with for nearly six years. The one I've told myself is forever off-limits, because our friendship is more important than any desires I may have for him.

Well, so much for *that* fucking resolution.

Raysen's voice cuts through the cloud of regrets and recriminations whirling around in my head. "Stay?" he says. His voice is soft and shaky, with a vulnerable edge to it that pierces me straight in my gut. "Please."

Someone places a hand on my shoulder, and I realize it's Dominic. He leans some of his weight onto me, calling my attention to him. "It's okay if you want to leave. But *he* really wants you to stay."

I shake my head, speaking to him in a whisper so Raysen can't overhear. "He doesn't *know*. Jesus, he thinks I'm a stranger, but I'm not, and—"

"It's my bad," Dominic interrupts. "I thought you knew what this was when I pulled you in. When it was clear you *didn't* know—well. I had a talk with Raysen. He knows. That's probably why he asked for the blindfold. He wants it, but he's scared."

I try to process everything Dominic is saying to me, but what keeps replaying itself on loop in my head are the words '*he wants it.*' And Raysen asked me to *stay*. He said *please*. I force myself to glance back down at him, still kneeling on the floor, face red and eyes covered, so that the feature most on display is his mouth. That soft, sensual mouth that's red and swollen, lips still shiny with a sheen of saliva.

He wants it.

My cock twitches as I recall the way the guy—*Raysen*—sucked me earlier, moaning around me and jerking himself off. Raysen *knew*, Dominic said. Raysen knew it was me.

The scent of Raysen's cologne drifts to my nose, and I can't believe I didn't notice it before. Probably because of all that thick cardboard in the way. Fuck. I smell it now, though. Swallowing, I shake off Dominic's hand and take a step forward. Another step, and then another, and I'm standing in front of

Raysen. I lower myself onto my knees, reaching out a hand to touch my thumb to the edge of Raysen's swollen bottom lip. I rub over the soft flesh, marveling at the way he opens for me, the way a barely audible moan escapes him at the touch.

He wants it.

"Okay," I tell him. "Okay, I'll stay."

II

RAYSEN

Logically, I knew there really wasn't anyone else it could be. Who else would come in asking for me by name, but who didn't know about the night's activities? It could only be Yuki.

Still, if I ever had any doubts, the second he said, "I've got to get out of here," I knew it one hundred percent. My best friend, the guy I've lived with for *years*, ever since freshman year of college—the guy I've been *in love with* for years—is standing in front of me as I kneel blindfolded on the floor, after having sucked off everyone in the room. Everyone including him.

Oh, God. I've had Yuki's cock in my mouth. Yuki's gorgeous, uncut cock, with its prominent mushroom head and ruddy coloring. Even if I didn't already know it was him, I would've recognized the scent of his body wash, woodsy and masculine and so distinctively *him*.

But I *do* know it's him. And he's kneeling in front of me now, the touch of his thumb on my bottom lip so maddeningly tantalizing that I can't help moaning out loud, parting my lips and silently begging for more.

"Okay," he says, "Okay, I'll stay."

A shiver runs down my spine, shock, arousal, and anticipation fighting for dominance inside me. I can't believe this is happening. Yuki is staying. Yuki's going to stay and watch me get fucked by all these men. Yuki is going to stay, and maybe, *oh God, please,* he's going to fuck me too.

"You still want this?" Dominic asks from somewhere above us, and I hesitate only a second before nodding. This isn't how I always pictured my first time with Yuki, but if it's my only chance to be with him, I'm going to take it.

Besides... There's something in me that wants to show Yuki this side of me and make him see me in a whole new light. Because this is me—the guy who gets off on being fucked by a group of men together, who loves sucking cock and swallowing cum. Not the boring roommate who spends most of his nights in, watching anime on Netflix. Not the guy Yuki's never once made a move on in the six years he's known me.

"Help me get him on the bed, then. He's been on his knees a while, so he's going to need support."

They pull me up by my arms, and my legs tingle and groan as I stand, but Dominic's done this many times before, and he's not a weak guy by any stretch of the imagination. Yuki isn't either. They get me on the bed without any noticeable effort, and I feel a palm on my chest, pushing me down until I'm pressed against the mattress.

A hand caresses down my side. I lose track of who's touching me, eventually, as hands roam over my body, followed by tongues and mouths.

"What can I do?" Yuki's husky voice asks.

Beside me, Lito answers. "Whatever you want, without hurting him. He doesn't like pain outside of hard fucking."

"And no cock in ass without condoms," Dominic chimes in. He grabs my wrist and places my hand over his half-hard cock, urging me to stroke. It's an awkward angle, but I manage to fall into a good rhythm fairly quickly. "He likes to be used, though. Lots of cocks inside him, in every hole. Loves being made to suck and lick and stroke. Don't you, babe?"

I whimper at his words, thinking about Yuki standing there listening to them. Yuki watching me be used. Watching how much I love it. "Yes."

"Fuck," mutters Yuki.

"You want us to show you how we play with him first? Get him nice and warmed up for you?"

Yuki's voice is strangled when he answers, but it's also laden with lust. "Yes. Show me."

Someone flips me over onto my stomach, then arranges me on my hands and knees. I think I hear Yuki groan at the sight, and I try to imagine how he must see me, naked and presenting my ass to be fucked. It's turning him on, and God, I love that.

Lube-slicked fingers probe my opening. One slips in, fucking into me in slow, teasing strokes that get close to my prostate but don't quite reach. Whoever it is begins to play with my balls, rolling them around in his other hand as he fingers me. Someone—I think it's Mitch—brushes the head of his cock against my lips. I open wide for him, and he slips inside.

As I suck him, someone else comes over and rubs his cock on my hollowed cheek. "Wanna see a fun trick?" he asks, and I know he's talking to Yuki. I also know what he has planned, and my spine tingles with anticipation and arousal at performing for Yuki.

Dominic laughs, which clues me in that he's the guy fingering me open. He adds a second finger, finally reaching for my prostate, laughing again when I moan and buck against him, my cock throbbing. "You're going to be amazed at just how wide he can stretch those lips."

A moan is all Yuki gives in answer, but that's enough. I slide my mouth off Mitch's cock and open even wider, tucking my tongue under my lower lip. They both groan as they press in together at the same time. It takes a bit of maneuvering, but eventually they find a rhythm, fucking my mouth in tandem as Dominic works me open with his fingers and teases my prostate.

"Lito, will you get the cock ring?"

"On it."

I shudder as I feel Lito sliding carefully underneath me to cradle my cock and balls in his hand. He slips the cock ring on with practiced fingers, then hums happily. "You look tasty all trussed up. I'm gonna help myself."

"Jesus Christ," Yuki mutters in a weak voice as I feel Lito's tongue on me, licking up the length of my cock and then between my balls. He trails down over my taint, then back up again, teasing the head of my cock.

"Nnngh," I moan, unable to say more, unable to beg, with the two cocks taking turns on my mouth.

Lito hums against my balls, swiping them with his tongue again. He places soft, wet kisses along my shaft and balls as Dominic works his thick, callused fingers into me. They work together on me for what seems like hours. Dominic deems me ready after a while, because he takes his fingers away, and the next thing I hear is the crinkling of a condom wrapper. Then he's pressing his cock into me, holding me down and sliding in deep.

Shivers break out all over my body as I'm filled in every hole and Lito continues to suck and lick me. It's almost too much, especially with Yuki here watching, and I want it to stop, but I also want it to never end.

Dominic doesn't go easy on me, especially after the good stretching he's given me. He rams into me hard, his balls slapping against my taint and making wet, smacking sounds as he fucks me.

"How is it?" Dominic says, grunting between thrusts. "You enjoying the show, friend?"

"Yeah," Yuki says shortly, his voice sounding strangled and gravelly, and I moan around the two cocks fighting for dominance in my mouth, choking a little when one of them thrusts too deep and triggers my thankfully-not-very-sensitive gag reflex. "I've never.... Fuck, the noises he makes."

"Yup," Dominic agrees, punctuating the word with a particularly sharp thrust that hits my prostate perfectly and elicits yet another desperate noise out of me.

They all take turns with me, rotating from my mouth to my ass, sometimes using my hands, sometimes just rubbing themselves against my cheek until I've got spit and precum everywhere. I shoot down Lito's throat at one point, pushing back against the cock invading my ass as I spurt over and over. I swallow another two loads, though I don't know whose they are, and someone comes across my back. The last is from Lito, who mutters dirty promises to me as he ruts into me hard enough to shake the bed.

Then it's over. I feel them each withdrawing slowly, leaving cool air in their wake. Dominic, as usual, is last to pull back. It's not long before I feel the customary warm washcloth scraping over my skin, cleaning away the spit and cum. But it doesn't end there like it usually does, because Yuki's still there, and Dominic's speaking to him in low tones I can't quite make out. Then he's speaking to me.

"You done, Ray-Boy?" he asks, stroking a hand over my forehead, smoothing down my hair.

I think about Yuki and his uncut cock sliding into my mouth. The taste of his cum. The way he groaned and bucked into me when he came. I shake my head. "More, please," I say. I want Yuki. I've always wanted him, and this might be the only time I get to have him. "Please."

"Shh," Yuki says, and places a hand on my chest, warm and steady. It makes me moan again, that simple touch, because it's Yuki, touching me after seeing all this. His voice is so gentle. He dips fingers into me, scissoring them, feeling how open I am. "Shh, baby. I've got you."

He takes his hands away and gathers me into his arms, rolling me onto my back. His weight on top of me is solid and comforting. I can feel his hard cock rubbing my stomach as he leans down to kiss my forehead. His thumb slides over the side of my face, brushing across my cheekbone, skimming the edge of the scarf.

"Can I take it off?" he asks me quietly.

I didn't think it was possible to feel so content and safe and *still* be this fucking scared, but I'm managing it. Up until now, I haven't seen Yuki's face, and it's kept this whole thing separate from real life. I *know* it's my best friend pinning me down to this bed, naked and hard and ready to fuck me. But if I'm not looking at him, I can *pretend* I don't know. I can cling to him and beg for him to fuck me, and be a whore for him, and then, if he wants, we can pretend it never happened. Not to the two of *us*. Just to some strangers at a sex party.

"Okay," Yuki says, probably sensing my hesitation from the way I've tensed up. His thumb glides over my lip again, a gentling touch. "Blindfold on." I can't tell if he sounds relieved or disappointed, and when he presses his lips to mine, I can't bring myself to care about anything but that he's kissing me.

The last—and only—time we kissed, we were in the first dorm room we shared in freshman year. We'd both ended up back at our room, tipsy and horny and lamenting the fact that we hadn't met anyone worth kissing at midnight. Yuki, his hair gelled back, wearing a shirt that was see-through and showed off the definition in his abs, cocked one eyebrow at me curiously, and, from the foot of his bed, beckoned me with a finger. I walked over, my heart pounding as he fisted my shirt and dragged me down for a hot, open-mouthed kiss. Then he pushed me back again, laughing.

"No," he said, "we really can't. I like you too much to fuck around with us. I'd have to find another roommate, and that'd be tragic. What would be even worse is having to find another guy as fun to hang around with."

At the time, it touched me that he cared more about being my friend than getting laid. In the years that followed, I struggled between regret at not pushing for things to go further than they did, and conviction that nothing really *could* have been better than where we've ended up—best friends, roommates, in it for the long haul. Yuki's become the most important person in my life, so it was good we didn't risk it all on one drunken night of fucking, right?

But *this*. This is different from then. This is the two of us, solid as cement, jumping into this thing together because we both want it. Fully aware of the consequences of our actions. Of what we stand to lose.

And God, it's terrifying. Even so, I don't want to stop kissing him right now. Not when I've been dreaming about this second kiss for years. Not when he kisses me like I'm something precious—like he loves me. Because he does. I *know* he does.

Just not the way I love him.

I deepen the kiss, making it wet and sloppy, moaning into his mouth—anything to distract from the thoughts I try not to let myself think, the feelings I can't afford to dwell on for too long. He rocks into me, his hard length leaving a trail of precum on my stomach. How many times have I fantasized about this? We didn't have four other guys watching us after having taken their turn with me in my fantasies, and I was never blindfolded, but I've been here before, in my mind. It's funny how similar fantasy and reality are—it was always Yuki on top of me, smelling like he smells now, tasting like he does, that I dreamed about.

Don't get sentimental, I tell myself, even though it's already too late. I need to put back the distance between us. I need to be the whore again, and Yuki just another guy I'm letting have his way with me.

I turn my head, wrenching away from Yuki's kiss. "Come on," I whisper. "Just fuck me. Fuck me."

Yuki utters a cry of frustration—or maybe it's arousal—that blows hot across my exposed neck. Then I feel him reaching down to roll a condom on, the smell of latex somehow wrong between us. I'm tempted to tell him—beg him—to leave it, but that would be stupid. That would be insane.

That would feel so *good*. So *right*.

Once he's sheathed, he just lines himself up and pushes, sliding in so easy he goes all the way to the root. It *still* feels right, even with the condom and the onlookers. Yuki's lips graze my jaw line, the smell of his shampoo and sweat scenting the air around me, both familiar and beloved. Yuki's muscles—the ones I secretly ogle whenever we go to the gym together—are working as he moves into me. God, and Yuki's voice.

"You're so tight," he mutters, voice shaking. "You're so tight and hot, and *Jesus,* you look so good. You looked good before, but *now*." He groans, his strokes losing all their finesse as he speeds up—*finally, finally, finally*—and fucks me like he owns me. I don't even have time to ponder over that '*before*,' because all I can concentrate on is the way Yuki's claiming me right now and how beautiful and broken and completely fucked up it all is.

"Yuki," I moan, forgetting that we're supposed to be strangers, that I'm not supposed to know his name, or at least not supposed to call him by it. He makes a wounded noise when I say it, like he wasn't expecting it either. "Want you in my mouth again. When you come. Want to swallow it." The back of my neck heats, my spine tingling with something that's probably shame, but maybe also a little bit of pride for being able to get the words out.

"Yeah," Yuki responds, rough-voiced. "I'm close. Fuck, I'm so close, Raysen."

"*Please.*"

He curses softly as he pulls out of me. I clench my ass, hating how empty is feels with him not there. The sensation-whiplash nearly has me keening. "Touch yourself," he orders, before his cock, still smelling of latex, presses into my mouth.

I swallow around him and curl my hand around my own cock, stroking furiously as he slides in and out, the weight of his cock heavy on my throat, rubbing against the roof of my mouth, stretching my lips wide with his impressive girth. Jesus, he tastes so good. I want his cum in my mouth again so much I could almost cry from the need.

I groan around my mouthful of cock as cum spills over my fingers, shuddering as my orgasm hits me so hard it makes my head spin and my vision go blotchy for a moment.

"Fuck, fuck, Raysen," Yuki groans, the rhythm of his thrusts going uneven as he tenses and pulses over my tongue, the taste of his spunk coating the inside of my mouth until he's all I can sense anymore—his taste, his smell, the feel of his body touching me in so many places, the hitch his breath as he rides through the waves of pleasure *I'm* giving him. *Me*. I suck him until he pulls away with a hiss, probably over-sensitive now that he's soft.

The scratch of a fresh warm wet cloth scrapes against my skin where my release is splattered all over me. I know it's Yuki cleaning me up this time, not Dominic, because of how the cloth moves, not perfunctory in the least. Yuki cleans me up like he wants to savor every second of it, like he's loving every cum-slick inch of my skin that he's cleaning.

And then the wash cloth's gone, and in its place—nothing.

The hum of the air conditioner, the air cold against my skin now that there are no naked bodies keeping me warm. Yuki's smell is still there, lingering on my skin *everywhere*, but I don't feel *him* anymore.

A throat clears. "Did he leave?" asks Lito, never one to beat around the bush. My stomach knots, and something like panic squeezes my chest tight.

"Shit," Dominic curses. "Stay put, Ray. I'll check on him." I hear his footsteps echoing down the hall.

"Fuck," I say. I reach up with shaking fingers and try to pull off the blindfold, but I tied it *really* tight earlier, and it refuses to budge. "*Fuck!*"

"Hold on, man. Let me help." Matt gently pushes my hands away and works on the knots. By the time he's got the blindfold loose and pulls the scarf away from my face, Dominic has come back into the room. There's a small smile on his face, which makes the tightness in my chest ease a bit.

"He's outside in his car. Across the street."

"Oh," I say, sitting up, wincing as my ass burns and aches in protest. "Did he—did say anything?"

Dominic shakes his head and lifts his hand—which holds my cell phone. "He told me to give you this. Said you forgot it in the car."

So that was why he came here. To give me my phone. Because I told him I was going to catch an Uber, and I couldn't do that without a *phone*. God, I'm such an idiot.

But would you do any of it different if you could?

I wish I knew the answer to that question.

I unlock my phone and pull up the text message that's waiting for me from Yuki.

Yuki: *I'll wait for you. Don't call an Uber.*

My heart races as I imagine the ride home with Yuki. It's

going to be just about the most awkward car ride ever. The thought of facing Yuki with my eyes wide open makes me want to go back into the bathroom and stay there forever.

Dominic puts a hand on my shoulder. "Sorry. It's my fault."

I shake my head. "It's fine. If it weren't, I would've told you as soon as I realized. But I was just—" Greedy. Horny. Lovesick. All of the above. Yuki has always been my Kryptonite, and I couldn't let go of the chance to have him, even if it was only an anonymous blowjob behind a DIY glory hole.

A hand nudges my arm, and I look to see Mitch holding out a pile of my neatly folded clothes. "You're shivering," he points out, nodding down to my still completely naked body. Yup. I'm not even sure it's from the cold, honestly.

I take my clothes and put them on, nearly losing my balance trying to get off the bed. Mitch steadies me, and I give him a grateful smile. I smile at all the other guys, too.

"Thanks for everything, guys. That was..." It was amazing. Being a slut for Dominic and his buddies always manages to take me out of my head and ease the sting of longing for Yuki, and we've entertained each other off and on for over a year, now. Even though I rarely see them outside of the activities we share within these four walls, they feel like friends.

"You're gonna have to tell us about him one day, Ray-Boy," Lito pipes up. "Because watching the two of you? Hot as fuck."

"And special," Matt says. "I mean, you're always amazing to look at, but with *him*, it's like you've melted down to the very core."

Couldn't have said it better myself. When it's Yuki, I feel like every part of me is an exposed nerve. It's intense and glorious and beautiful. It's scary, too.

"You'd better go," Dominic says, leaning in to kiss me on the cheek. "Don't keep your guy waiting too long."

My guy. I wish that were the case.

Dominic must see what I'm feeling in my expression, because his face softens and he pulls me in for another kiss, this time a soft, chaste brush of our lips. I think it's the first time he's ever kissed me like that. "It'll work out," he promises quietly. "I have a good feeling about this. Now go."

Yuki's car is waiting across the street, just like Dominic said it was. My heart beats so fast as I approach it almost feels like it's trying to jump out of my chest. Yuki looks up when he notices me passing the driver's side to go around to the passenger's side. I'm *so* tempted to open one of the back doors and curl up on the seat, so I don't have to face him. I don't, though, because we *do* need to talk about this. I might as well get it out of the way.

Yuki doesn't say anything when I first climb into the car, though his gaze flicks over to me for a second before turning resolutely back to the windshield. He starts the car and begins to pull out of his parking space.

I clear my throat. "Thanks for waiting."

Yuki makes a noncommittal noise in the back of his throat and flips on the radio.

We make it all the way home without speaking another word to each other, with the radio blaring loudly. I glance at the clock and notice that it's not even midnight yet. God, it seems like an entire lifetime ago since I left the apartment.

Yuki parks in his usual space and turns off the engine, but he doesn't open his door. Instead, he turns to me, meeting my gaze for the first time since the ride began.

"You seemed pretty familiar with those guys."

Okay, not *exactly* what I was expecting him to ask, but not far off the mark? "Yeah. Uh. I guess you could consider all of us friends. The kind who fuck."

Yuki lets out a humorless laugh. "Yeah, I kinda got that. Jesus, Raysen. How many times have you done that?"

I don't know if I can answer. It's not always all of them at once. It started out with a Grindr hookup with Lito, who introduced me to Dominic as a possible third, and it spiraled out from there. "Not very many times like this. This was a one-time thing. Usually it's only threesomes, and never with the, um."

"Glory hole?"

My face heats. "Yeah, that."

"But you liked it." I try to find an ounce of judgment in Yuki's voice, but there is none. "What am I saying, of course you liked it. You were into it the whole time."

"Yeah, I liked it. I mean, being fucked out of my mind by four hot men? What's not to like?"

"Five," Yuki reminds me.

"Right." I let out a sharp exhale, my spent cock valiantly twitching in my jeans at the reminder that Yuki fucked me too. "Did you like it?"

Yuki's eyes find the windshield again. He squints at the car parked in front like it's the most interesting thing in the entire world. His hand grips the steering wheel he's still hanging onto, white-knuckled. I don't even think he's aware how hard he's gripping it. I hold my breath, waiting for his answer.

"Is it wrong that I liked it?" he asks in a low voice. "I shouldn't like watching you like that. Watching you take all those things they did to you."

"It's not wrong. I... I liked it, too. You watching me." Okay, maybe that's too much. God, I sound like such a sap when I say it I'm almost afraid Yuki will realize how much he means to me. How much I liked it because it was him. How the kisses we shared, the way he held me and took care of me, were my favorite parts of the entire night. Those little touches were what made the night the best of my life.

I can't tell Yuki any of that. I'm not brave enough yet. I don't think I'll ever be. What if I lose him? Now that my mind isn't hazy with arousal, I have to admit that it was a bad idea to give in to temptation. This one night with him really wasn't worth potentially ruining our friendship.

"Are you going to do it again?"

"What?" For a moment, I think he's asking me if I'm going to be with him again. But then he clarifies.

"That. With Dominic and those guys. You going to do it again?"

My shoulders slump in disappointment, and it's a good thing Yuki still isn't looking directly at me. "Um. Probably. It's..." A good distraction from everything I'm not allowed to have with Yuki. "... fun. Lots of fun."

Yuki's hand uncurls from around the steering wheel. He flexes it a few times. "Good. I mean. It's a good thing you're having fun. You don't date enough." He gives a short laugh. "Although I guess you don't need to date if you're having orgies left and right."

"It's not that often." Only when I really need it. Only when I'm especially lonely. Only when I'm pining for Yuki and can't seem to get the thought of pursuing him out of my head.

"They're safe, at least?"

"Yeah, you saw the condoms they used. Dominic plans everything and makes sure everyone gets tested. They're all good guys. I considered dating Dominic at one point, but he's kind of got the same issue I have and—" I stop, realizing what I've just said.

"What issue?" Yuki asks, honing in on the important stuff right away.

The issue of being in love with someone he can't have and not being able to truly fall for anyone else. That issue.

"Nothing. It's not—I really can't talk about it. It would violate Dominic's privacy." Not actually a lie. I don't think

Dominic would give a damn, but that doesn't make it okay to tell Yuki all about his business, right?

"Okay, sure. What about the other guys?"

I shrug. "Lito's not really a commitment sort of guy, and Matt and Mitch are together. They're open and they like to play around, but they're not really looking for a permanent third, and it's not really what I want anyway."

"Oh."

"Any more questions?" I ask him.

"So many more."

I laugh. "Yeah, fair. But let's get to all your questions when I've showered?" I'm feeling pretty worn out, and I've still got lube trying to leak out of my asshole. I just want to crawl into bed and process what happened tonight.

"Yeah, okay."

We both leave the car and walk back to our apartment, Yuki walking a little ahead of me, his shoulders visibly tense. When we're inside, Yuki makes straight for his bedroom. "I'll shower in the morning," he calls over his shoulder. I stand by the hallway, watching as his bedroom door closes shut behind him.

"Shit," I mutter. "Shit shit shit." I walk to the bathroom and close the door, stripping my clothes off and stepping under the shower. I hesitate as my hand grabs the shower handle, remembering how Yuki touched me all over, how drops of his sweat had hit my naked skin as he fucked me. I don't really want to wash it away, even though I really *do* want to, because four other guys have sweated and jizzed all over me too, and I don't have very much sentimentality where they're concerned.

Shit, this is crazy. I can't believe I've become one of those people who don't want to wash themselves because someone's touched them. *Get a fucking grip, Rainey.*

Due to my distraction, I forget to jump aside when the shower switches on, and I yelp as the cold water hits me, summoning goosebumps up to the surface of my skin. It only takes half a minute for it to get warm, though, and I hastily jump back under the spray. The warm water feels good against my sore body. I clean everywhere, paying particular attention to my ass, which is swollen and puffy from all the use it's had tonight.

Pressing my fingertips to the opening, I close my eyes and recall the way Yuki's arms pressed around me, the small hitches of his breath each time he slammed his thick cock into me. I'm too exhausted to get fully hard again, but a frisson of arousal shoots through me at the memory.

Yuki's bedroom door is still closed when I come out of the bathroom. I consider knocking on his door, but I don't want to wake him if he's already asleep. The existence of his 'so many more' questions burns a hole in my mind. I want to know what he was going to ask. I want to know what he thinks about all this. I want to know if he felt anything other than lust when he watched me and fucked me and held me like that.

I want to know, but I'm too scared to ask the questions myself.

III

YUKI

December 30th

I get into my car and turn the ignition, sighing as I lean my head back against the seat. I should be happy that the work day is over, but right now I don't know whether I'm looking forward to seeing Raysen again tonight or dreading it.

Things have been kind of awkward between us, and it's all my fault. I was the one who spent all day Sunday holed up in my room, pretending I was too immersed in Martha Wells' writing to go out into the living room for anything more than a quick snack. By the time I finally snuck out to make dinner, Raysen was already in his bedroom and didn't seem like he was coming out anytime soon. The bathroom smelled of his shampoo, and all I could think was that I wanted to hold him close enough to smell it on his skin again. The skin I'd touched like I owned the whole of him only the day before.

But I wasn't supposed to think those thoughts about my best

friend, and I shut it the fuck down. I've been shutting myself down pretty much constantly ever since.

As I near the apartment building, my eyes automatically find Raysen's parking spot. He works at a local game development company that's only a ten-minute drive away from our building, so he's usually home before me. Except his car *isn't* parked in the stall. The stall isn't empty, either. There's another vehicle where Raysen's tiny maroon Ford Focus usually is. The large blue truck *does* look somewhat familiar, though. Wasn't there a blue pickup truck parked outside the house on Sunday?

As I approach, I notice that there are people in the car. It doesn't take a genius to guess one of them must be Raysen. Raysen and one of the guys from Saturday's activities.

Before I can even decide how I feel about that, the doors open, and Raysen steps out of the passenger's seat. On the driver's side is, of course, Dominic. He's the first to spot me, standing like an idiot on the sidewalk a couple of yards away from them. His mouth curves into a pleased smile, and he lifts his hand to wave at me, saying something to Raysen.

Raysen turns his head and watches me as I walk up to them. The setting sun picks up the highlights in his hair and makes it glow a deep, burnished gold, and my chest aches at how beautiful he looks.

"Hey," I say. "Where'd your car go?" Because asking the obvious question of "*what is Dominic doing here?*" is kind of beyond me at the moment.

"The auto shop."

"Oh." That's right. I feel like shit, realizing I forgot all about the fact that Raysen's car is crapped out. How did he get to work this morning? I could've given him a ride if I'd pulled my head out of my ass long enough to notice.

"Dominic towed me with his truck and gave me a ride home."

"That's nice of him." I try to shoot Dominic a friendly smile, but I don't know if I manage to make it look natural or not. This is all so awkward. Dominic's wearing a worn construction T-shirt which shows off his buff arms, and he's got worn jeans on. It looks like he's just come from work. Of *course* the guy would be a sexy construction worker.

"Yup," agrees Raysen. "He's great." The smile *he* gives Dominic is all warmth and affection, and I feel a spark of jealousy that it's not directed at me. "Thanks, Nicky."

Dominic nods. He steps back and looks between the two of us. "You kids figured shit out yet?" Neither of us says anything for so long that he just laughs. "Well, I'm having a party at my place tomorrow night, if you want to stop by."

"A normal party?" I ask.

Dominic's eyes sparkle with amusement. "Yeah. Food and drinks. Some music. I'll even put the TV on for the countdown to midnight."

"Sounds fun," Raysen says quietly. "Maybe I'll see you there."

"How about you, handsome?"

"Maybe," I say, unable to outright refuse. Something about the commanding way Dominic's eyes hold mine tells me he doesn't get a lot of outright refusals. Being with Raysen in that house again doesn't seem like it's going to help me with my resolve to stay away from him, though. I clear my throat, my cheeks flushing as he continues to study me. "I might have plans."

"Well, keep us in mind if you end up having a free evening. I promise it's a 'normal' party this time."

"Right."

Dominic makes his goodbyes to us and drives off in his big truck, leaving us to stare as he departs. We walk in silence the rest of the way to the apartment, which isn't unusual for us.

What I like about Raysen is that silences with him are usually nice. Sometimes we spend entire days in the apartment lounging on the couch together, saying not one word to each other but simply going about our own tasks. Because it's Raysen, though, it's good. Peaceful.

Peaceful isn't exactly the word I'd use to describe our silence today. Tension seems to crackle in the air. We've barely said ten things to each other since Saturday night. I know it's my fault for avoiding him the past two days, but as soon as we got back to our apartment and I was confronted with the entirety of our lives, I chickened out.

Out of *what*? I still don't know. I just know that when I saw our fridge with all its magnets from the many trips we've taken together and the postcards Raysen's parents send us every time *they* take a trip anywhere, addressed to "our favorite boys," I was reminded of just what I stood to lose if I pursued this—whatever it is. So I ran into my room and hid there like a coward.

Now things are weird between us and I just want them to go back to how they were before, when I only allowed myself the occasional glance at Raysen's ass. When I didn't know how good it felt to hold him in my arms and work my cock into his tight hole.

"You're attracted to him," Raysen says just as we get back to the apartment.

"Who?" I ask, confused.

"Dominic."

"Isn't everyone? *Look* at the guy."

Whatever answer Raysen wanted, it wasn't that, because he frowns and looks toward his bedroom door like he wishes he were in there again. "I'm just surprised. He's not really your usual type."

"I don't really have a type."

Except you.

Where did *that* come from? But it's the truth. From the moment I met Raysen, I was attracted to him. The years of living together, of sharing our hopes and dreams and sorrows, have only made me want him more. The trouble is, it's also made it more impossible for me to really have him. I'm the kind of guy people dump. The kind of guy you fool around with for a few weeks or a few months, and then move on from. That's always been fine for me with other people. But the thought of having something like that with Raysen and then having him move on from me?

Fuck, I don't think I could take it. Not for all the brain-meltingly hot blowjobs in the world.

I inhale deeply, preparing myself to talk to Raysen. "So Saturday night..."

"Saturday night."

"It was a—"

"What were those questions?" Raysen cuts in.

"Huh?"

"I asked if you had any other questions that night in the car. You said, I quote: 'so many more.' And then you just fucked off to bed and never asked me any of them. So what were they?"

I make my way to the couch and sit down, picking up a book from the side table and opening it at a random page. "I can't remember."

A blatant lie. But what am I going to say? *Does it always take multiple guys to satisfy you? Is that why you almost never date? Do you want to do that again with me? Was it as amazing for you as it was for me? Could you ever lo—*

"Really? We're going to go with memory loss?"

I close the book, unable to pay attention to any of the words. Sighing, I look up at Raysen, who's standing right in front of me, his arms crossed over his chest. Closed off. Upset. Sexy as fuck. "Doesn't matter. All those questions—they come down to one thing, and that thing is something that we shouldn't do. You mean too much to me for me to throw it all away just because—" *Your body is fucking heaven. Your mouth is hot and your ass is tight and the moans you make when I'm fucking you...*

Lost in my thoughts, I don't notice how Raysen's moved forward, how he's suddenly towering over me, his hands curling around my neck and pulling me forward as he bends down and kisses me. I kiss back, throwing myself fully into it, my tongue pushing into his mouth, tasting, testing, swallowing up the little noises he makes in the back of his throat. He climbs onto my lap and I place my hands on his hips, holding him close to be sure he doesn't fall. We kiss and kiss and kiss. Just like Saturday night, like that other night, so many years ago, his kiss melts me. Kissing him is like coming home.

How have I never realized that?

"Who said anything about throwing it all away?" rasps Raysen, when we pull apart. His mouth is red and swollen from kissing and his eyes are glassy, and he looks almost exactly like he did that night, when the cardboard barrier came down and he was kneeling there, naked and wanting. Except now, I can see his eyes, bright and pleading. "I don't want to throw anything away. I want to keep it all." He kisses me again, nipping gently at my bottom lip. "Think about it."

With that, he climbs off my lap, the crush of his body on me a weight I miss more than I ever thought I would. He walks into the bathroom and slams the door shut. After a moment, I hear the shower come on again. Fuck, it feels like I'm always sitting here, listening to the shower go off in the bathroom, trying to stop myself from jacking off to the way Raysen's shampoo smells. This is ridiculous.

'Think about it,' he said. It's all I've *been* thinking about for days, and I'm still no closer to an answer than I was when I started. I want Raysen, and he wants me. But is it worth it? Will

I be enough for Raysen in the long term? When he gets tired of me, like everyone else does, will we be able to go back to being *us*?

When Raysen gets out of the shower, I expect him to confront me again, but all he does is go into his room to change into the usual T-shirt and shorts he lounges around the home in.

"I'm going to order pizza," he announces, padding into the kitchen to pour himself a drink of water. In another minute, I can hear him on the phone, ordering a large pizza with pepperoni and mushrooms on one half and Italian sausage and pineapple on the other half. It's the order we always split when both of us are too lazy to cook. It's normal. It's us. Which I guess is the point he's trying to make.

Or maybe he just wants pizza.

I go back to my book as Raysen comes to sit on the couch next to me and flips the TV on. We sit there in silence that slowly grows more and more companionable until the pizza arrives.

"I'll get it," I say, and get up to answer the door. Raysen's browsing through Netflix when I come back with the pizza, setting it on the coffee table in front of us.

"Have you seen this?" he asks, nodding to the current selection on the screen, something called *I Am Mother* with the picture of a robot on the cover. "I've heard it's good."

"No," I lie. I *have* seen it, but if Raysen wants to watch something together after spending two whole days basically not hanging out, I'm going to watch it with him. Besides, it *is* a good movie.

We sit on the couch, eating pizza and watching the movie, and it's almost like every other Monday evening at home together, except there's a noticeable two inches of distance between our bodies on the couch, when usually we're fighting for leg room, limbs criss-crossed over one another. I'm only half paying attention to the screen; the other half of my mind is fixated on whether Raysen will come over and kiss me again. Or whether I'll have the courage to make the next move.

The movie draws to a close without either of us having moved from our positions. Raysen glances over at me as the credits roll. "Well, *that* was an ending."

"Yup," I agree. "Did you like it?"

"Yeah, I kinda did." He stretches, long arms reaching up toward the ceiling, his head tipped back so his Adam's apple is on display.

The impulse to lean over and lick a line down the length of his exposed neck and suck on the jut of his collarbone is strong. He's always turned me on in a vague, nebulous way, but now that I know what he looks like when he's coming around my cock, I can't seem to stop picturing him like that. Can't seem to stop wanting to touch him, and draw out more of those dirty, needy noises from his lips.

"I think I'm going to head to bed," he announces, eyes not quite meeting mine but hovering on my face. "Unless you..." He trails off, biting his lower lip. I'd think he was trying to tease me if I didn't know him better than that. All these gestures to draw my attention to his mouth are unconscious.

I can't resist. Inching closer to him, I reach out with one hand and touch that lower lip, running the tip of my thumb along the edge. Raysen sucks in a sharp breath. I close my eyes, tensing when he moans and opens his mouth to let my thumb dip in, until I feel the heat of his tongue on it. "I don't think I can do this with you," I tell him.

I take my hand away. He swallows, and there's hurt in his eyes that wasn't there before. I want to take back what I said just to get it to disappear, but I don't. This is way too important. This is my heart. This is our fucking friendship. Our *home*. Because Raysen's not just my best friend—he's home. That's why kissing him feels the way it does. Because he's been *home* for ages.

"You're my best friend."

"Okay," he says, his voice barely above a whisper. "I get it. I guess I'll... go off to bed now."

"You don't have to—"

"I'm tired. Work was boring as hell today. I'll um. I'll see you tomorrow." I nod, watching as he stands and makes his way back to his room. I remain on the couch for a few more minutes, my heart still pounding, my cock still half-hard simply from the touch of his mouth on my thumb. Have I just fucked this up more than before?

December 31st

Raysen's already dressed by the time I get home, in a nice blue button-down and black jeans that make him look good enough to eat. He left before I could get to him this morning. Not that I had much to say that I hadn't already said the night before. And now, apparently, he's on his way out.

"You going out?"

He shrugs. "I thought I'd drop in at Dominic's party. Since he invited us."

Of course it'd be to Dominic's party. Of fucking course.

"Okay," I say, trying my best to sound casual. I don't know if I succeed or not. Part of me wants to grab Raysen and demand that he not go. Or just *grab* Raysen, period.

"Are you staying here?"

"I don't know. Maybe I'll go out." *Find someone to help me get over you.*

But as soon as I think those words, I dismiss the idea. No. The problem is I don't even *want* to get over Raysen. At least not in that way. I'd love to *be* over him again, the way we were at Dominic's, sliding into his ass, watching as he loved taking it.

"Well, if I don't see you again, remember we've got brunch with Mom and Dad and the whole crew tomorrow at ten."

Now I'm going to have to look Raysen's parents in the face during New Year's Day brunch after having gang-banged their son. Perfect start to the new year. "I'll be there," I promise, because I don't miss family brunches if I can help it. Having been kicked out of my family for being gay, Raysen's parents are pretty much the only parents I still have left.

Which is why I *shouldn't* be thinking about gang-banging their son again. I can't lose them. I can't lose Raysen.

Raysen casts a soft, melancholy look my way, then grabs his wallet and keys from the kitchen counter and leaves.

I spend half the night sulking by myself, starting and abandoning half a dozen things on Netflix before giving it up. The festivities are already starting, with fireworks sounding in the background every so often, even though it's nowhere near midnight yet.

Thinking about midnight makes me think of Raysen, surrounded by a bunch of hot guys, Dominic included, all of them potential kissing candidates when the clock strikes twelve. As much as I tell myself it's a bad idea to do this with my best friend, I can't help wanting to be there, too. Wanting to be the guy he chooses to kiss in the first minute of the new year.

I've hopped into the shower, changed, and walked out to my car before I even know what I've decided. It doesn't take much to remember the exact turns to take to get me to Dominic's place. It's half past eleven when I pull into a parking space on the street and walk down to the house. In contrast to Saturday night, the door to the house is left open tonight, with a screen door allowing music and light to stream out. I hear laughter and conversation coming from inside, too. It *should* be an inviting atmosphere, but I still pause outside, unable to let myself in.

I'm saved from my dilemma when the door swings open, nearly hitting me in the face. Dominic, one arm carrying a large trash bag, blinks at me for a moment. "What're *you* doing here?" he asks.

"You invited me."

"Yeah, I know, but—" He huffs out an annoyed breath. "I just sent Raysen home with Lito."

"Oh," I say, my heart sinking. I guess Raysen's found someone to kiss at midnight after all. Fuck, why did I come here in the first place? What did I think was going to happen?

Dominic swears softly, letting the screen door shut behind him with a loud slap against the doorframe. "Not what I meant." He tosses the large trash bag onto the lawn outside and turns to me, rubbing his hands over his jeans. He's in a dark button-down shirt that molds to his muscled chest and arms perfectly, but I don't even take much time to admire him because my head's full of thoughts of Raysen going off somewhere with a guy who isn't me.

Dominic's hand claps my shoulder, shaking me a little. "Hey, man. Snap out of it. I said, that's not what I meant. I sent Raysen *home*, to *you*. Or at least, to see if you were still there. Lito had to drive him since his car's still in the shop, remember?"

"*Oh*," I say.

Dominic laughs shortly. "Yeah. Oh. Goddamn, you should've seen your face. You looked absolutely crushed." He shakes his head. "I don't understand it. If you're so gone on him, *why* was Raysen getting wasted earlier tonight and telling me he's got no chance with you?"

"I'm not—"

"Don't even try to deny it. I saw your face right now, remember? And I saw how you looked when you were with him the other night. You couldn't look away from him, not even for a second." Dominic steers me around the side of the house as he speaks, pushing me down onto a bench propped against the wall. "So tell me. Why *can't* you be with him? Is it because of what happened with all of us? Because you know we're nothing compared to you, right? He'd drop everything in an instant to be with you."

I shake my head. "No, it's not that. I don't think I'd have a problem with it if it's something he wanted, you know? It's not like I've never had a threesome before."

"Did look like you were enjoying it, in the moment," Dominic said, eyes glinting with amusement. "But then you disappeared on us as soon as it was over."

"Didn't think there was a post-orgy powwow I had to be a part of."

"Well, there usually is. It's called aftercare. You might want to look it up."

Way to make me feel like an asshole. But I deserve to, if I haven't done what I needed to for Raysen.

Dominic bumps against me, his elbow nudging my side. "Don't look so guilty. It's fine. We handled it, and you didn't know. But yeah, look it up later. For right now, Raysen's at home, probably thinking you fucked off somewhere. He's been moping all night about you. Tell it to me straight. Do you want him?"

"Isn't it obvious I want him? You saw us together."

A huff of frustration. "I'm not asking you whether you want to fuck him. Who *doesn't?* What I'm asking is whether you *want* him, Yuki. Because he wants you. He's wanted you for years."

"You don't know that." Dominic *couldn't* know that.

Dominic shakes his head, a small secretive smile playing on

his lips. "You know the reason why he plays with us like he does?"

"Am I supposed to know?"

"It's because he wants to distract himself. He told me it was difficult to watch you with other people. Kept wanting you for himself, and it was torture for him. So yeah, he enjoys being fucked out of his mind and made to be a slut for a group of guys. The reason he *needs* it, though, is because you're on his mind, and he told me you would never be interested in him. 'Permanently friend-zoned' was the phrase he used. He's wrong, isn't he?"

"We *are* friends," I say. "We're best friends." That doesn't stop me from wanting him. I've already admitted to myself that it never has. The revelation that Raysen has been struggling with the same thing is as reassuring as it is scary.

Except it's not *attraction.* Raysen hasn't just been attracted to me, I realize. He loves me. Which is fucking lucky, because I love him, too.

"Friends can be lovers," Dominic says, but there's a bitter note to his voice that doesn't make any sense. And to be honest, I don't really care at the moment.

"I need to get back home." I need to get back to Raysen. Now more than ever, being in the same room with Raysen when midnight strikes for the new year is absolutely necessary.

I jump off the bench, and Dominic comes with me, clapping me on the back as he walks with me out to the front again.

"Don't speed. There's still plenty of time to get him."

"Thanks," I say, and I really mean it. Sure, Dominic has fucked Raysen in front of me, but he feels more like a friend than a rival. If Raysen's been having a hard time because of me, then I'm glad Dominic and those guys were there to help him through that.

"No thanks needed. I like Raysen. Not as much as I wish I

liked him, but I guess that's a moot point now that you're in the picture. And you kind of always were."

"Yeah," I say. "Yeah. I'm always going to be there." No matter what else changes between me and Raysen, that never will. I was a fool to think anything could make it. There's nothing to be afraid of. Raysen would never leave me, because he's Raysen. The guy my world has revolved around for over half a decade. Raysen is there to stay, and so am I.

When I get back to the apartment, Raysen's not in the living room and the bathroom door is slightly ajar, with no light coming from inside. That leaves, by process of elimination, Raysen's room. Except when I push open his door, the bed is empty. My stomach sinks. He should be home by now, right? Or maybe he's with Lito somewhere.

And it would serve me right, wouldn't it? I had my chance to go with him to the party, and I didn't take it. My jaw clenches tight, and I palm my phone, swiping up to Raysen's number on the recent calls screen.

Raysen's ringtone sounds from somewhere outside. I quickly follow the noise, hanging up as I realize it's in the kitchen.

"What the..." I stare at his phone on the kitchen counter for a moment, then practically trip over myself on my way to my own bedroom as realization dawns.

I pause in the doorway, taking in the sight of Raysen on my bed, facing the wall, the steady rise and fall of his body indicating he's already asleep. As I step closer, I realize that he's clutching my pillow to his chest, and has half his face buried against it. My chest aches as I stare down at him, looking so heartbreakingly vulnerable sleeping in my bed.

He shifts when I get into the bed and curl my arm around him. "You're back," he says, voice still raspy with sleep.

"Shh. It's fine. Go back to sleep."

"What time is it?" His hand comes up to touch the arm I have wrapped around him, but he doesn't push me away. "Is it midnight yet?"

"Not yet. Soon, though."

I trail my hand from his stomach up to his chest, marveling at the fast thud of his heart underneath my touch. He's nervous. Just as nervous as I am. "You're back early."

"So are you."

I should tell him about going to look for him at Dominic's, but I'm distracted by the delicious smell of his hair. I can never resist that citrusy smell. And being this close to him, I can also smell a faint hint of his cologne. The special one that I bought him for his birthday. I bend my head until my nose touches the back of his neck, and breathe in the scent of his skin. His breath hitches, muscles shifting under my hand.

"I didn't want to be out. At least I didn't really want to be out by myself. I was just so damn frustrated with you. Shit. I think I'm still a little drunk. Not supposed to say all this to you."

"Why not? You can be frustrated with me if you want to. Hell, I'm frustrated with myself." I slip my hand down again, traveling past his abdomen and reaching under the hem of his T-shirt to touch the skin. "Raysen... Turn around."

I feel him freeze when my fingers skim over his stomach, but it's only for a few seconds. His eyes are heavy-lidded when he finally turns to face me, either from sleep or from alcohol; I'm not too sure. They're still beautiful, though.

"I love you."

Raysen's beautiful eyes go wide, some of the haziness clearing before melting into a more tangible confusion. "What? Fuck, I *am* drunk. I thought you just said–"

"I love you. I *love* you. I don't know anyone who I love as much as I love you. I don't think I've ever allowed myself to, because you were always there. Maybe that makes me an asshole. It's probably why things never worked out with everyone else, now that I think about it. I thought it was just me being impossible at relationships. Well, I guess it's me. But it's you, too." I know I'm rambling, but I don't even care. Normally I would be more worried about how much like an idiot I sound. But right now? All I care about is the man in my arms, gazing at me like his whole world has just been turned inside out.

"If you're joking about this, I'm going to punch you." His voice is whisper-quiet. I have no doubt he means it.

"Not joking." Before I can say more, the sound of distant fireworks pierces the quiet of the room.

"It's midnight," Raysen says.

"Yeah," I reply. "About time. I've been waiting all night."

"Waiting for what?"

I smile, reaching up to cup his face. "To do this." I tilt his chin up and press a soft kiss to his lips. I intend for the kiss to end quickly, but Raysen makes a noise of protest and chases my lips, stealing a second kiss from me, this one deeper and lasting much, much longer.

We kiss and kiss as the sound of fireworks echoes around us, and for a while there is no thought in my mind except for Raysen's lips and tongue, his mouth taking all I have to give. I could go on kissing him forever, but I'm distracted by his hand on the waistband of my jeans, his fingers undoing the buckle of my belt.

"Fuck. We can't," I say, though it pains me to refuse him. There's nothing I want more right now than to fuck the hell out of him. I want to be inside him again, this time without anyone watching us. With both our eyes wide open.

"Why?" Raysen asks, his voice nearly a whine, the undercurrent of a tremor audible in it.

I sigh, grabbing his hands and bringing them up to my mouth to kiss. "You taste fucking delicious, but you also taste like gin. I don't want to take advantage of you." I remember Dominic said he's been drinking all night. Trying to drown his sorrows, I guess. Because I've been such a fucking idiot.

"I don't mind being taken advantage of."

"I know." I recognize the growl in my own voice, but I can't help it. I remember just exactly how well Raysen took to being taken advantage of. It's not really helping me regain any of my self-control.

Raysen must take my words in the wrong way, because in the next instant he looks nervous, biting his lip and dropping his eyes. "Do you hate it?"

"No. I already told you I don't." I reach up and touch his lower lip, hooking my thumb into his mouth until the pad rests on the tip of his hot tongue. "I can't hate anything about you. I loved taking advantage of you. I loved watching, too. You were so fucking hot." And beautiful. Always beautiful.

"I thought you were jealous earlier tonight. When I was going to go over to Dominic's. And yesterday, too."

I grin. "Oh, I was. You told me you tried dating him. I thought maybe you were trying again. I wouldn't blame you, not when I was being stupid about things. When he told me he sent you home with Lito, I was pretty worried too. I don't mind the sex, because it's just sex. But the other stuff..."

"Hold on a minute. Dominic's? You went over there?"

"Just after you left, apparently. I had a little talk with Dominic." My hand trails down his neck, my thumb pressing into the hollow above one collarbone, feeling the rapid beat of his pulse. "He told me you've been in love with me for years."

"He told you that? Fuck."

"Hey. There's nothing to be embarrassed about. I'm glad he told me. That was when I realized it's the same for me. I've been in love with you for years and never even realized it."

Raysen huffs out a laugh, touching his forehead to mine and placing his hand on my shoulder, clutching me to him. "Christ. I feel like this must be some wonderful dream that I'm going to wake up from any second now. All my wishes have come true and it's terrifying. Tell me I'm not dreaming."

"You're not dreaming. Or at least, if you're dreaming, then we're both dreaming together."

"Being in the same dream with you doesn't sound half bad. Are we having sex in this dream?"

"No, we're not having sex right now. Under the influence, remember?"

"We're not driving. It doesn't matter."

I consider saying that *he* may not be driving, but I certainly will be. Into his hot ass. Over and over and over again. My cock, already hard, twitches against Raysen's stomach, and he utters a soft moan.

"I know exactly what you're thinking," Raysen says. He probably does, too. We've always been in-sync.

"What's the capital of Sweden?"

Raysen blinks at me. "Huh?"

"I'm testing how drunk you are."

He laughs, his body shaking in my arms, his breath warm against my lips. I tilt my head to catch him in another kiss. Soon he's rubbing against me, creating friction that shoots pleasure up my spine.

"Stockholm," he gasps. "Stockholm is the capital of Sweden. And it's been an *hour* since I've had anything to drink. I went home because I missed you, not because I was drunk off my ass. Surrounded by hot guys who want to fuck me, and all I could think about was you off hooking up with a random at a club somewhere."

"I never went out. I just stayed home and moped about *you* going out."

"We're both idiots. Kiss me again."

I give in, holding him close and kissing him hard and deep, our tongues sliding together. When Raysen reaches for my belt buckle again, I don't stop him, just help him undo it as I work on his clothes. Soon we're naked, our breaths coming in short gasps as our hard cocks rub against each other, hot and silky-smooth.

"I knew it was you," Raysen says in-between increasingly desperate kisses.

"Yeah?" I don't even ask him what he means. "You asked me to stay."

"I suspected when Dominic told me there was someone here who asked for me by name. Who else even knew I was there? So I was about ninety percent sure it was you. Then you spoke, and I *knew*. I didn't want you to go. I didn't want to pass up the chance to feel you inside me. I was so scared it would fuck everything up, but I couldn't resist."

Some part of me is *still* scared it'll fuck everything up, but kissing Raysen like this, *holding* him in my arms like he's mine, is worth all the fear in the world. "I want inside you."

Raysen groans as I kiss him again, sliding my tongue in deep, fucking his mouth with it. "Yes," he hisses. A helpless moan escapes his lips when I push him into the mattress and climb over him. "Yes. Fuck me."

"Supplies in the nightstand?"

He nods, and I open the drawer and reach inside for lube and condoms. I pause when he asks me, "Have you been with anyone since Gray?"

"No," I answer confused.

"And you've been tested since, right? I know you had an appointment the other week."

"Yeah," I say. My cock twitches again, my eyes widening as I realize where Raysen's going with this.

"Everyone got tested before the, um, party. Plus the condoms. So it's not one hundred percent, but I'm pretty sure I'm good to go."

"You want me to go in you bare?" I ask, my voice more of a growl than anything else. I've never done it raw with anyone. I always thought I'd do it when I met someone I could trust, and it's never quite happened. But I trust Raysen. And apparently, he trusts me.

The look on Raysen's face is so full of need that it knocks the breath out of me for an instant. "Yeah. Just us. No barriers."

"Fuck," I mutter, hurrying to kiss him again. I can't get enough of him. I'm fairly certain I never will.

I work him open, using plenty of lube but going quick, listening to his satisfied grunts as he takes each finger. His hole is hot and soft around my digits, and it flexes greedily when I find his prostate.

"*Yuki*," he says, and it occurs to me he hasn't said my name since the last time I was folded over him, working my cock inside him as his body went lax with pleasure. It's even better, hearing him say my name like this while he's meeting my gaze, his blue eyes clouded with lust. "It's good. So good. Just— Come on. Please. *Fuck me*."

I pull my fingers away and smear more lube over my cock, lining myself up. "Ready, baby?"

Raysen nods, moaning as the head pushes into him. It's so unbelievably hot and tight without the condom. Even better than the pleasure of going in bare, though, is the knowledge that this is us. *Just us. No barriers*.

"I'm not going to last," I say. "You feel so good." Even with the limited prep, he's opening so easily for me. His cock jerks against his stomach as I slide in all the way, not pausing until I've bottomed out.

"So good," he repeats, panting the words, clenching around my cock and sending electric thrills of sensation through me. His face is flushed, and his eyes are bright as he stares up at me. They're full of wonder and love, and I know I'm giving the same look back. "So hot. Making me so full."

I groan, starting a rhythm of push and pull into his body, leaning over to kiss him as I move. "You like being full of me?"

More nods. "Love it. Love *you*. Yuki, please. *Fuck* me." Just as I intended, I drive into him, harder and faster than before, nearly dizzy with pleasure as he takes me in again and again. Each of my thrusts rips a noise from him—moans and gasps and pleas for more. I give it to him, bent over his body, kissing and nipping at his mouth, our bodies slapping together, creating more noises from the intensity of impact.

He tenses, mouth falling open as he comes, his release pulsing between us. His ass squeezes around me, milking my cock. I give myself over to my own orgasm, pumping my cum into him, staring into his eyes like I wanted to do the last time we were together.

"Oh, God. I can feel it," he rasps. I moan and take a few last thrusts, thinking about my cum filling him up.

"Take it all, baby," I tell him, kissing him again. It's slower and sweeter this time, something soft now that the hard edge of urgency has left us. "Love you."

"Stay?" he whispers. There's nowhere else I want to be right now—*or ever*—and no condom to get rid of, so I settle beside him, my softening cock slipping free from his body. I press a kiss to his forehead and gather him into my arms, not caring that we're both covered in cum and sweat.

Mine, I think. *You're mine, and I'm yours.*

I wake up tangled in Raysen. He's still asleep, his dark hair falling over his face and obscuring his eyes, his mouth slightly open. He's so beautiful I feel my breath catch at the sight. All my fears from the past few days, from all the years we've been friends, seem to have melted away. All I can feel right now is love and contentment. The rightness of Raysen being in my arms is undeniable. Why did we wait so long, and why did I try to fight it so hard?

My phone rings, and it takes me a moment to figure out it's in the pocket of my jeans, which are still on the floor. I try to extricate myself from Raysen to answer it without waking him up, but I don't succeed. Raysen stretches and yawns, making a small noise at the back of his throat that has me wanting to kiss him again, morning breath and all.

Phone in hand, I reach for him. Before we can kiss, though, I glance at the phone screen and stop short. "Your mom's calling," I say, showing him the phone, which has *Mama Rainey* as the incoming call.

Raysen groans. "*Brunch.*"

I swear softly, answering the phone with a slightly sheepish, "Hello?"

"Yuki? We've been waiting, and Raysen isn't answering his phone. Are you boys okay?" I feel a surge of fondness for the woman who practically adopted me when my parents kicked me out in sophomore year of college after finding out I was gay. Of course she'd be worried about both of us. I know Mary Rainey thinks of me as a second son, just as I think of her as the mother I wish I had.

Which makes this situation hella awkward. "We're fine. Sorry, Mama. We overslept. Headed out now."

"Just tell them to order first?" Raysen rasps, close enough to be picked up on the other end of the line.

"Is that him?" Mama Rainey asks. "Sounds like he just woke up. Are you two... *Oh.*"

Here's the point at which I put the phone on speaker.

"What's going on?" I hear Raysen's dad, Raymond, ask in the background.

Raysen clears his throat, shooting me a panicked look before speaking. "Uh, sorry. We're running late. Can you guys start without us?"

"Late night?" Mama Rainey's voice is *just* light enough that I *know* we're made.

"Do you hate it?" I ask, just as lightly, even though inside my heart is beating double-time.

"Oh, Yuki," she says, sounding *so* disappointed in me. "How can you ask that when it's the best news I've heard all year?"

Beside me, Raysen laughs at her play on words. "Dork," he says.

"That's where you get it from," I quip, and he grins and kisses me on the cheek.

"Sorry for being late, Mama. We'll get changed and meet you guys."

"Oh, don't worry about us," she says breezily, sounding like a cat who got the cream. "Just take your time, darlings. We'll see you soon."

Raysen grins at me when I hang up, his hand smoothing over my naked side. "So. I guess the cat's out of the bag. If you wanted to keep this" — he gestures between the two of us — "a secret, I'm afraid you're out of luck."

I smile back at him, leaning in to take that kiss I wanted from earlier. "I don't feel unlucky."

We jump into the shower together and wash off all the sweat and cum dried on our bodies. I sink to my knees and take Raysen's cock into my mouth, tasting him for the first time. As I suck him, my fingers find his entrance and brush over it, feeling the slippery slide of lube and cum leaking out as I breach him with one finger. He cries out as he comes down my throat, and then he sags onto his knees beside me and kisses me, tasting himself on my tongue.

He returns the favor, his mouth just as hot and talented as the first time. I'm practically wobbly on my feet after, though I do manage to get changed into new clothes. I extend a hand to him as we exit the apartment together; my entire body sings with joy when he slips his hand into mine.

"What should we tell them?" he asks, just as we get to my car.

I shrug. "That I own your ass now?" I meant it as a joke, but as soon as I say it, I think about how I claimed Raysen's ass not twelve hours ago, and how I can't wait to fill him up with my cum again as soon as we get home.

"Accurate," he says, the heat in his gaze making it obvious he's thinking very similar thoughts. He licks his lips. "But maybe something less crude. My sisters are gonna be there, remember."

"Right." Raysen's sisters are all under the age of sixteen and are still, miraculously, innocent as lambs. Just thinking about them makes me want to go out and buy a shotgun so I can threaten boys not to mess with them. "Think *they'll* hate it?"

"I think they'll all start planning our wedding as soon as we officially tell them we're together."

The talk of wedding plans should be scary, but all I feel is a giddy happiness I can't really control. "Together, huh? I think I like the sound of that." We're *together*. My best friend and I are together.

Raysen smiles. "Me too. They're going to want to know how it happened, though."

"Yeah, 'I found out I loved him when we fucked for the first time at an orgy' doesn't have quite the right ring to it."

"Glad you can joke about it." Raysen tilts his head curiously at me. "You *really* don't mind?"

"I didn't." I shrug. "I might mind now that we're 'together.' But it was sexy as hell, and if you wanted to do it again... I mean, I wouldn't want it every other week. But... I dunno."

"Maybe. It was fun and, yeah, sexy as hell. But I really *did* do it because I needed to get my mind as far away from you as possible."

"Did it work?"

"Sometimes. Not always."

I put my hand on his thigh as I steer us down the street toward the freeway. "You won't need to get me off your mind now."

"Nope." I catch his grin for a split second before I have to focus back on the road. "It's unreal. You have no idea how long I've loved you."

"Six years?"

He laughs. "Nearly. God. I wanted you from that very first kiss in freshman year. But you were so adamant you wanted to be my friend."

"I did. And I don't regret it." All those sci-fi movies we stayed up late watching together; the many bad matching Halloween costumes; the time Raysen held me all night while I tried very hard not to cry when my parents disowned me; the joint celebration his family threw us when we both graduated university; all those meals Raysen heated up for me while I was trying to pass the bar exam—I'd never trade our years of friendship for anything. "But I'm glad we're here now. I'm glad you're mine."

"I'm yours," Raysen agrees.

I smile, looking forward to the next six years, and the next, and so on—and all the new memories we'll make together, as best friends *and* as lovers.

EPILOGUE - RAYSEN

February 15th

"ARE you sure you're okay with this?" I ask Yuki for what must be the twentieth time as he dries his hair after the shower.

Yuki laughs, giving my ass a playful swat as he passes me on his way to grab clothes out of the dresser. "As long as this ass is mine, I don't care about anything else." He turns back to me, cocking an eyebrow and then closing the distance between us to grab me by the chin. He kisses me, his tongue pushing past my lips. "This mouth, too."

A shiver of arousal runs up my spine, and I melt a little into his arms. "Everything. All yours."

"Then yes, I'm definitely okay with going to Dominic's party with you. Looking forward to it, in fact."

I take a deep breath, nerves and excitement warring for dominance in my mind. When Dominic texted the other night to invite us, we were curled up on the sofa rewatching *Firefly*, and Yuki had glanced over curiously as the message notification sounded. I half expected him to get jealous, but I guess whatever he and Dominic talked about the night we officially got together helped them bond. I'm glad, since Dominic's become a friend to me, even if I did kind of hide the friendship from Yuki at first.

When we get to Dominic's place, the house is decked out in gaudy Valentine's Day decorations, and there are fairy lights in glass jars hanging from the pergola in the yard. There are also about twenty other people hanging out all around the house, including a few I recognize from one or two other parties I've attended here.

Dominic greets us both with a hug when he spots us, taking his time with Yuki and whispering something into his ear that I don't catch. Whatever it is, it makes Yuki grin and mutter a "Thanks" back.

"What did he say to you?" I ask when we're alone in the kitchen getting drinks.

Yuki pauses as he selects a bottle of cream soda from the fridge. "He said it's a kink-friendly crowd here tonight, so I should feel free to 'stake my claim' on you if I feel like it."

My breath hitches in my throat and my cock throbs with sudden arousal at the idea of Yuki taking me the way he did our first time together, with a bunch of people watching.

Yuki steps closer to me, crowding me up against the kitchen counter, his hands on my hips, thumbs digging into my flesh and crotch pressing close enough for me to feel the hard-on underneath his jeans.

"You're into it," I say, a little shocked and a *lot* turned on.

Yuki lowers his mouth to my neck, sucking on a spot just beneath my ear. "I *did* tell you I thought it was hot. I wouldn't mind doing it again."

"Not the sharing me part." I don't think I *want* to be shared. Being with other guys because I was missing Yuki is one thing. Now that I have him, I don't really *want* anyone else.

"No, not the sharing you part. But the fucking you while

people watch us? The showing you off, so everyone can see just how fucking gorgeous and slutty my boyfriend is? Yeah. *That* I want to do."

I moan, my cock ready to burst out of my underwear at Yuki's words. Every time he calls me his boyfriend, I get this small, secret thrill inside. I still can't believe that after all those years of being in love with Yuki, he's finally mine.

"I want to show you off, too," I admit. "Want them to see how good you make it for me." I only discovered how much of an exhibitionist I am when I met Dominic. For a while, it bothered me that it was something I had to hide from Yuki. Now it seems as though Yuki is as much of an exhibitionist as I am.

Yuki pulls me into a kiss, plundering my mouth with his tongue and leaving me breathless in his wake. "Where?" he rasps, and I moan as the reality of this settles upon me. We're actually doing this. Right now. Tonight.

"Anywhere you want." As long as Yuki's with me, I don't care where it is. "Although I suppose we should go find somewhere that's not the kitchen."

"Okay, then. Let's go."

We wind our way through the house, with Yuki's arm curled around my waist, his hand crammed behind the waistband of my jeans, kneading my asscheek. We get a few laughs and smiles as we pass people I know. No doubt they've noticed the raging hard-ons pressing against the fronts of our jeans.

We're told Dominic is in the room at the end of the hall, the one we were in for the glory hole scene. When we knock on the door and are told to come in, we find him sitting on a chair facing the bed with his jeans open, stroking his cock as Matt and Mitch sixty-nine on the bed. When we catch sight of the three of them, Yuki's hand clamps down on me, squeezing my ass tight. I'm not surprised this turns him on. Matt and Mitch are gorgeous together.

Dominic cocks an eyebrow at us. "Are you two going to close that door, or are you just here for a looksie?" he asks.

Yuki moves us more into the room and swings the door shut behind us. "Okay if we hang out here?"

Dominic grins. "You guys need a hand, or you just looking for an audience?"

"Just an audience," I answer for us.

"But maybe we'll watch the show first," Yuki says, wrapping his arms around me from behind and pushing his hard cock against the small of my back. "Get ourselves ramped up."

We remain there, with Yuki leaning against the door and me leaning against him, both of us watching Matt and Mitch pleasure each other while Yuki's hands work to undo the zip of my jeans.

"No belt or underwear," Yuki hisses into my ear. "Were you hoping for this, Raysen?"

I moan and push back against the hot length of his cock, wanting it inside me already. In either one of my holes. In both. "I wanted to be ready, just in case. You've been hinting ever since we got the invitation. *Teasing*."

On the bed, Mitch arches his back with a loud groan and pulls out of Matt's mouth, his cum jetting across Matt's face and chest. Matt, muttering something under his breath I can't catch, grins widely before reaching up to gather the cum and push it into his own mouth as Mitch continues to suck him off.

"Fuck, that's sexy," Yuki murmurs. He scrapes his teeth along the side of my neck, and tingles bloom from that spot, reaching all the way down to my fingertips.

"You can do it to me if you want," I tell him quietly. "Come all over my face."

"Yeah, definitely another time. Tonight I want to come inside you." As soon as he says it, the image of his hot cum dripping from my used hole as everyone looks on fills my mind, and

I know he's thinking about it too. I shudder again, then moan when he takes my cock out and pumps me.

"Everyone's going to see it," I mumble, arching into Yuki's touch.

"You want that, baby?"

I nod slowly, watching as Matt's orgasm overtakes him and he jerks up into Mitch's mouth, body spasming. I can see Mitch's throat working to swallow it all.

Soon they're sitting up and rolling off the bed. Dominic, cock still swaying in the air, stands to pull clean sheets out of the closet, and the three of them quickly work to strip the bed and change the sheets. It'd be faster with four people, but neither Yuki nor I want to stop what we're doing right now. Yuki's hand is rough on my cock without lube, but it's still so damn good I can't help leaning back against him and thrusting into his grip.

"Bed's ready, Ray-Boy," Mitch calls out. "Damn, you two are hot. Guess it's probably no use asking if you want a helping hand or four?"

There's a sharp slapping sound, with Mitch's yelp following quickly after. "Greedy bastard," Matt says, laughing. "I dare you to get it up again right now."

"Give it some time, baby."

"I already asked while you two were too involved with each other to notice," Dominic says. "The answer is no."

"Can we still stay and watch?" This is from Matt again.

Yuki answers for both of us. "Yeah. That's kind of the point." He leads me to the bed and stops when we get to the foot of it, then helps me out of my clothes. My skin feels hyper-sensitive when the fabric drags across it as the clothes come off. Yuki gives a low hum of approval when he nudges me to turn me around so I'm facing Dominic.

Dominic grins up at me from his seat on the chair, stroking his cock idly as his eyes caress over my body, from my face down to my hard, leaking cock. "This your way of displaying to me what I can look at but can't touch, Yuki? And after I was so kind and helpful."

"This is me giving you a good show *because* you were so kind and helpful," Yuki responds. He kisses the side of my neck and pumps his hand on my cock for a few seconds, squeezing out a shiny bead of precum from the tip. "But you're right. You can look, but you can't touch. Yeah, Raysen?"

I nod, and Yuki kisses my neck again.

"Come on, baby. Let's show them who owns your ass."

He starts by making me get on my hands and knees on the bed, then pushes me down until my face is pressed against the mattress and my ass is up in the air. Once I'm sufficiently spread, he kneels behind me, and I feel his hot breath over my hole just milliseconds before his tongue is licking into it.

I don't even try to keep in the sounds that spill past my lips as Yuki rims me, eating my ass like he's starving and I'm the only meal he's going to have this entire week. As is always the case when we're together, everything else fades into the background and he becomes my sole focus. Hell, it's been that way even before things got physical with us. Maybe it's always been that way.

He fingers me open, and I wonder if he uses lube, too, because he's definitely sliding more than one in there at a time. It could just be that I'm primed for it. I *want* Yuki's cock in me. I always want it.

"Hurry," I pant. I can't help the small push of my hips against him. "Please."

But Yuki doesn't hurry. He takes his time finger-fucking me, stretching me out until I feel like I'm going to explode just from the way his fingers are filling me.

"Jesus, Raysen. You're so hot." He takes his fingers away,

rubbing his cockhead over my hole, the heat of it making me moan against the mattress.

"Want you," I say, my voice still somewhat muffled, but clearly audible enough, because Yuki *finally* begins to push into me. After over two months of sleeping together, this still gets me emotional. I love the feeling of Yuki's hands on my hips, gripping me to pull me closer as he sinks his hot length inside.

Yuki sets a slow rhythm, letting me get used to his cock with slow, lazy pumps that are just shy of hitting my prostate. It keeps me from hurtling over the edge, hanging on to the sensation of being filled over and over again.

Eventually, though, things pick up. Yuki hauls me closer, pressing his chest against my back for a moment, shifting our positions on the bed so the angle is *perfect*. Soon I'm crying out with every thrust he makes.

"Love you," he whispers, his lips trailing to my neck to plant soft, warm kisses there, punctuating each of his thrusts. "You feel so good."

"You too," I manage to say back, though my voice is so shaky and slurred with lust I'm not sure the words even come out. It doesn't matter, because it must be obvious to Yuki. He curls fingers around my hard cock and strokes me, each glide of his hand stoking the fire burning inside me. "Oh, God."

"Can't wait to feel you squeezing me when you blow it, baby," he murmurs, his hand speeding up, working me into a frenzy of pleasure. I arch into his touch. My body vibrates as it readies itself for release. I'm a whimpering mess, bucking against Yuki, chasing the pleasure of heat and friction connecting our bodies. I'm so close. *Almost*.

"Yuki. *Yuki*. Hold me," I say, desperate for more contact as my orgasm speeds toward me.

Yuki hunches over me and puts both his arms around me. For a moment I miss his hand around my cock, but the heavy, warm weight of him on me is even nicer. That, coupled with the proximity of his harsh, hitched breaths right next to my ear, sends me flying. I clench around him, crying out as he milks jet after jet of cum from me with his hand.

"Fuck, Raysen. Yeah, just like that," Yuki mutters.

I collapse in a heap, Yuki's arms trapped under me. He doesn't seem to care, because he continues to whisper sweet, dirty praises into my ear as he drives into me, driving me into the mattress with movements that are getting more and more uneven. "I love you. So perfect. All the noises you make. Are you still loving it?"

I make a noise in the back of my throat, acknowledging a fact we both already know. I *really* love it. Even after my own orgasm, my body is thrumming from the high of fucking, just waiting for the moment when Yuki comes and I can feel his seed in me, slicking me up.

"*Raysen*," Yuki huffs out, the word devolving into a moan as he gives another hard thrust and then stills, his cock pulsing inside me. He stays there for a while plastered over me. He's breathing hard, the rhythm of it matching the beat of his pulse, which I imagine I can feel all over my body.

I turn my head to the side so I'm not trying to breathe through the mattress and sigh contentedly, closing my eyes. Above me, Yuki chuckles.

"Happy?" he asks, shifting some of his weight off me and pulling. I immediately feel the warm trickle of his cum sliding down to pool on my balls.

"Mm-hmm."

There's a low murmur of voices, but I'm so out of it I can't tell who it is or what they want, just that there's a brief increase of background noise when the door to the room opens. Then it's closed again. The quiet comes back, and I can hear the thump of my own heart again.

We doze in the bed for long enough that by the time we get dressed and go outside, half of the people who'd been milling around in the living room have either gone or found a private room somewhere. My limbs feel loose and tingly in the best way, and I can't wait to get home and collapse into our bed. Dominic is on the couch, though, his arms around a cute twink with spiky purple hair, so we stop to check in with him.

"Sorry we stole your room," I tell him, flashing a sheepish smile. "We think we probably owe you new sheets, too."

Dominic waves my concerns away. "It's the mattress I'm worried about, so as long as you didn't somehow go through the waterproofing on the sheets we're good." He grins at us. "Thanks for letting me watch. It was fantastic. Mitch and Matt said to give you a thumbs-up, too. I think they're banging another one out in the laundry room right now."

Several people chime in with teasing remarks about their regret at missing "the show." I glance at Yuki to gauge his reaction. He's blushing and grinning at the same time, answering friendly questions with only a hint of shyness. After a few minutes of light conversation, we say our goodbyes and head to the car.

We drive with the windows rolled down and the wind buffeting our hair. Yuki's quiet, but that's okay because the radio's playing Queen's "Don't Stop Me Now," and it's kind of the perfect end to a raunchy evening.

Yuki takes my hand and holds it on our walk home from our parked car. He shoots me an oddly shy smile. "That was good. Right?"

I smile back at him. "It was good. I loved showing everyone how good we are together."

Yuki nods. "It felt like a celebration." He laughs. "That's lame, huh?"

"No, that's fair. It kind of did. Like we were celebrating each other, and everyone was helping us do it. Thank you."

"Thank *you.* I'm the luckiest guy in the world. It was fun. Hot." He squeezes my hand in his. "The best part is I get to go home with you."

I stop, tugging on Yuki's hand to pull him closer for a soft, slow kiss. "Yeah," I say, staring into the eyes of my best friend and the love of my life, "that's the best part for sure."

— The End —

Want to be notified when Dominic's book comes out? Sign up for my newsletter or join my Facebook readers' group.

THANKS FOR READING!

Dear Reader,

Thanks so much for reading *My Best Friend's Secret*. I hope you enjoyed this story, which was originally part of a multi-author "Glory-ous New Years" short story giveaway on Prolific Works. I added 5,000 words to the original novella to give more insight to these characters before, and I hope it left you feeling satisfied. If you enjoyed this story, consider picking up some of my other works on the next page. For news and updates on upcoming releases, please follow me on any of the social media accounts below. I've already got Dominic's story in the works and I can't wait for you to read it. Do come find me and let me know if you are interested in reading about any of the other guys in the infamous glory hole scene!

For access to ARC opportunities, bonus content, and special giveaways/promos, join my facebook readers' group (https://facebook.com/groups/lacybits) *or* subscribe to my newsletter (https://crystal-lacy.com/subscribe).

facebook.com/crystal.lacy.author

twitter.com/writerlacy

instagram.com/writerlacy

goodreads.com/writerlacy

bookbub.com/authors/crystal-lacy

amazon.com/author/crystal-lacy

ALSO BY CRYSTAL LACY

The Oahu Lovers Series

Brave for You

Change for You

Ready for You

Stand Alone Titles

Holiday Fling

Kissed in Paradise

My Best Friend's Secret

Vanilla Steamer (*part of the Bold Brew series*)

Brother-in-Law Material

ACKNOWLEDGMENTS

Thanks to Abigail Kade and Lynn Michaels for putting together an extremely fun exchange that spurred me to write the first version of this story. Also thanks to my other fellow participating authors for helping me stay excited about this project, especially Kyleen Neuhold and Lynn Van Dorn, who were kind enough to listen to me ramble about my story lol. Thanks to Eden for being supportive even though glory holes isn't her thing, and thanks to Tai for helping me proof this as well as Davina for providing the final proofing. You're all lovely and I couldn't do this without you <3

www.ingramcontent.com/pod-product-compliance
Ingram Content Group UK Ltd.
Pitfield, Milton Keynes, MK11 3LW, UK
UKHW042002190726
13854UKWH00005B/2129